SWEETEST NOTHINGS

A Collection Of Poetry & Prose

CAMERON LINCOLN

ISBN: 1523342842
ISBN-13: 978-1523343843

DEDICATION

For the ones who inspired me, and the ones I may inspire in return.

CONTENTS

FOREWORD

This is a book of curiosities, of poetry and prose, short and longer, strange tales from a mind rarely made up. There is light and shadow; swift encounters and dark deeds; steampunk spies and love in the world of superheroes; campfire tales and the sweetest nothings.

I very much hope you enjoy them.

Thank you to Jenna Dixon, for her patience and precision in editing, for calling me on bad habits, and for the support of a saint.

Thank you to Rebecca Sherwin, Rachel Brightey, Jo Curtis, KL Shandwick, Zoey Hart, Cecily Bonney, and Lisa Fulham, for endless belief.

Thank you, dearest readers, for taking the journey with me.

THE GIRL

The girl enjoys the chaos,
  the bedlam and misrule.
She sometimes plays the goddess,
  and oftentimes the fool.

She's a notch on endless bedposts,
  and carved a few herself.
She's been the rose and thorn,
  the cure and the ill-health.

She smokes because she likes it,
  and drinks because it's fun.
She owes no explanation
  to any judging one.

Her life's a crumpled roadmap,
  of a journey without end.
Pleasure is the compass,
  the route is hers to bend.

ALBION

She dreamed.

Or perhaps, in this unknown place, she remembered.

The uncertainty was not troublesome. Sounds were muted, as if heard underwater. She felt womb-encased, warm and safe, but knew it would not last. She thought of birth.

She recalled it as one does a night time reverie, fleeting and ephemeral. It was blinding, lancing oblivion's black iris, tasting of salt and copper, smelling of scorched metal and umbilical, anodyne musk. Her newborn lungs expelled plasma-laced saline and stung at oxygen's first assault, vocal chords stretching fervently with a scream that would remain nested in memory like a hungry, prowling beast.

Gears ground somewhere, engines whirring and tabulating, ratchets working with fine precision. It was the sound of London and half the world, a white noise that few noticed. In her half-lucid state she recalled pistons and steam, a sense of floating.

No. Not that. Flying.

*

The market children were playing Albion.

The girls fought over who was to portray their heroine and the boys debated who was to be her latest dastardly villain, or eager companion.

Her name was everywhere: adorning the paste-spread bills on the city's soot-caked walls, calling for her true identity; on the pages of its best and worst news rags; on the lips of dock workers, street peddlers, aristocrats and doxies, from the heart of the city to its farthest outskirts; in the eager, fertile minds of the children who re-enacted the adventures found in their penny dreadfuls. Albion: the greatest daughter the Empire had ever known.

Abigail O'Hare watched them dart and duel before her as they weaved their way through the bustling marketplace in Earl Square. A young girl in a pair of cheap goggles, the lower half of her face covered in her best approximation of Albion's alleged attire, a red velvet scarf tugged snug over her mouth, and the two subordinate boys, chasing her with sticks. She grinned; even if they were to examine her closely, they would never recognise her, never know they were so close to the object of their delight. Even if she were to tell them, they were not likely to believe.

She perused the avenues of collapsible lean-tos with their haphazard canopies, stalls laden with jewelry, clothing and trinkets in every conceivable colour and shape. She savoured the sounds of barking vendors and the smells of world cuisines stewing and sizzling, then drifted into

Archie's Eyes.

She strode into the covered shop to the clink of her boot spurs. It was a trove, partitioned into sections with ornately decorated Chinese shades, each one filled with rotor-spinning displays of fine spectacles, microscopes, telescopes and sturdy but stylish goggles custom-made for a dozen trades. She examined a pair of ornate theatre binoculars until his avuncular tones came from beyond the nearest partition.

"It took three days to carve and set the lenses, young lady, and three more to hand-gild the shell, yet I don't fathom there's time enough left this century to craft a pair befitting a lass of your calibre." She followed his voice to find Archie Munroe, faultlessly dressed in a crisp white shirt and braces, hunched over a cluttered work table with his concertinaed-metal eyeglasses perched on his aging, bird-like nose. "Though I must say, at the risk of appearing un-gentlemanly, the spurs have got to go."

"These were given to me by Lincoln Vaughan himself," she said with mock indignation. "It's rare for him to give anybody a gift other than a bullet between the eyes."

He took her hands in his and kissed them with a noble flourish. "A face like yours could charm a skyboat off the deck without a single drop of water in its heart."

She fished into the satchel slung at her hip and pulled out a pair of brass goggles with a fine leather strap. One of the black lenses was scuffed, the other completely cracked into spiderwebs. He took them with the look of a parent whose child had returned from a day's play with a skinned knee and bleeding nose.

"Oh, what have you done to *these?*" Archie pondered, picking at the lenses with a pair of fine silver pliers.

"Not I," she said. "A redskin's tomahawk."

He looked wistfully at his creation, now nothing but broken remnants. Then, with perceptible indifference, he tossed the goggles over his shoulder and pulled a replacement pair from a drawer in his scratched, scorched desk. She held them up to examine them in a thin shaft of light streaming through a hole in the roof slats.

"So how long shall you grace Britannia with your presence?"

"Frontiersville now reaches the far shores of the Americas," she told him, securing the goggles in her bag, "and the last resistance in the Crimea is gone. I serve Victoria until she says otherwise. I read the new edition, by the by, as soon as I stepped off the boat this morning."

Archie rocked back in his seat with a creak of wood and bones, raising a wizened white eyebrow. "And?"

"Fantastic as ever," she smiled. "You always make her far more fearless and wonderful than I ever could. And I shall have the diaries for the next edition to you as soon as they have been appropriately censored by her majesty's agents."

"Alas, we are lucky it is not the Empire's secrets that sell the tales, my dear, merely her spirit of adventure. No amount of my florid prose can ever truly capture the nation's heart if you weren't allowing it to beat." Archie slid open a drawer and handed her a pristine copy on the crispest paper, the print without a single smudge. "First copy off the press. I know it thrills you."

The artwork on the cover displayed the sloping rooftop of Big Ben and the midnight sky beyond, London a mere scrawl of streets and lamps far below. Silhouetted against the full moon was Albion, poised nimbly in defiance of gravity, a sabre in one gauntleted hand, a sleek pistol in the other, the weapon and her masked face angled towards the approaching enemy, a Russian skyboat bristling with lightning cannons.

As she flicked the pages she saw, in her peripheral vision, Archie straighten in his seat, and she sensed him hold his breath. She stole a cursory glance over her shoulder, long enough to identify the two new arrivals as Belmont's men. Matching red bow ties and moustaches; the fool made them groom themselves to a uniform standard to impose an air of menace. Abigail found the look laughable, but Belmont was not one to hire clowns.

"Miss O'Hare," the first one said icily. "A word in your most delicate ear."

They would have guns: wrist-strapped single shot pistols that could fire at the simple slap of the forearm. They were armed as they were dressed: without diversity. Two of those shots to the back would be enough to fell her in seconds. She held her tongue a moment longer.

"Now, now, boys," Archie said, levering himself from

his chair with a cane, wheezing as he did so. "Miss O'Hare is shopping. Surely you're both world wise enough to know what a bad idea it is to interrupt a lady with an open purse."

"Quiet, Munroe," the second sneered. "Miss O'Hare. We require that you step outside."

Abigail had remained flicking through the fiction digest throughout the whole exchange. She now put the paper in her satchel and dropped a number of coins before him. "A pleasure as always, Archie," she said and took a step backwards. The goons did the same with great caution, prepared for the pounce of a tigress.

"Stay in front of us, Miss O'Hare, there's a good girl."

"This is a dreadful misunderstanding, sirs – " she began as they emerged into the sunlight and the noise and bustle of the marketplace. "What do I call you?"

"Call us what you like, it matters not one jot," the taller one said.

"Vant and Parker's easier, though," the shorter and clearly less intelligent of the two said. "Leastways we'll know which one of us you're talking to."

"Then do tell, Mr. Vant," Abigail asked with an angelically innocent, ladylike lilt. "Where might we be going, and who exactly do you think I am to be taking me there?"

"Mr. Belmont wants to speak to you," Vant explained.

"And you can bloody well drop the performance," Parker spat. He was watching her with the concentration of a wrangler waiting for a cobra to strike.

"I don't know who you think I am – "

"You bloody well do," Parker sniped. "We don't think, we *know*. That steam-powered, penny-dreadful dame on her majesty's service. I don't care what that crusty old writer gives you to do in the pages of those rags every month, you're nothing but a cut-throat in a corset." Parker sounded genuinely aggrieved, as if the mere notion of a hired mercenary was anathema to him; hypocrisy was still not sitting well.

But they *knew*.

Weightless insects rolled in her stomach. *How* they knew, she could not be sure until she spoke to Belmont. She considered for the briefest of moments making a scene, but they may fire instantly and vanish amongst the ensuing chaos as she bled to death surrounded by panicked vendors. "So where are we going?"

"Your father's workshop," Vant informed her. "Mr. Belmont should be there presently."

"Excellent, I'm sure we can straighten all this out," she said with as much poise as she could muster, despite the sickening flutter in her gut, now that she realised her father was in immediate danger. If these bad breed had truly unravelled the mystery of Albion, the likelihood that her mother's dress shop in Crawcrook Street would be swarming with mercenaries was exceedingly high.

The playing children darted in front of her, rushing to a stall run by a matronly Indian woman tending sizzling pans of curried chicken, where they harmlessly threatened her with elaborate death if she were not to feed them at once. The woman smiled and started dishing up small bowls of browning leftover rice.

"My dear girl," Abigail called to the child in the Albion costume.

The girl and her companions gave her their attention. Vant and Parker shared an uncertain glance.

"Miss O'Hare – " Parker began, as Abigail fished in her satchel.

"Yeah, wot?" the girl demanded with enough appropriate attitude that Abigail felt strangely proud.

"I just wondered if you might be interested in this," she said, presenting them with the first edition of the latest *Astonishing Adventures Of Albion.* The three children hesitated.

"That's the new one!" the taller of the two boys gushed in awe, his rice forgotten.

"Give it 'ere!" the shorter of the two said. The tiny Albion lunged before the boys could, desperate to reach it first.

Abigail pivoted and tossed the magazine. It sailed between Parker and Vant, who realised too late they were about to be assaulted by excitable youths. The children squeezed through the narrow gap between them; Albion reached the magazine first and dashed off with her friends in pursuit.

Abigail seized the opportunity, lunging for the curry

stall, clamping the thick wooden handle of a spitting skillet, dropping to her knees with startling alacrity, hefting the contents backwards over her head. Parker and Vant were turning back to face her. The lumps of chicken did little, but the rain of burning oil spattered them and drew screams. The crowd gasped and the Indian woman shouted something in her native tongue.

Parker blindly slapped his oil stained sleeve and a small thunder crack echoed through the market; a smoking hole opened in the wrist of his jacket and a strident *pang* of metal on metal was all but lost amidst the sudden noise of the crowd.

Abigail took a second to register the indentation on the spice-streaked pan raised between her face and Parker's shot, then bounded the three strides to her attackers. She swung a buffalo-hide boot into Parker's groin, doubling him over. Vant, skin ruddy and promising to blister with ugly relish, was preparing to spend his own shot. Her free hand went to his sleeve and wrenched his arm skyward, the skillet slamming against the concealed pistol and discharging it hopelessly at the clouds. She brought the burnished metal down swiftly across the bridge of his nose, then on the upswing caught the hunching Parker under his chin. Both of them fell at her feet without another movement.

The market patrons and store owners had overcome their initial shock and were watching the scene with the expected surprise of typical Londoners. Little shocked them, and never for very long. She placed the dented skillet back onto its hotplate and offered her apologies to the store vendor; the woman looked both awed and a little put out, a situation smoothed over with the handing over of enough coin to pay for the poultry and a new pan.

Archie limped up through the dispersing crowd. "Are you hurt?"

"No. But they know who I am, and if that's the case they know you're my unofficial biographer. Be careful." She kissed him quickly on the forehead, then spun on her heel and broke into her fastest sprint.

The dress shop was empty, mannequins standing in silent elegance, draped with hand-sewn gowns and corsets her mother had slaved over, the way she slaved over Albion's adventure-scuffed outfits. Abigail rattled the locked door.

She barrelled along the road as fast as her boots would carry her, scattering pedestrians, urchins and gentry, all barely able to register her as she whipped by. Steamsled pistons hissed as carriages braked and swerved to avoid her. She was aware only of the danger her parents were in, of her need to reach them. The threat of their whole world unravelling was now an immediate, occurring truth.

Her father's workshop sat on the edge of the docklands, a half mile from the meandering Thames; the work Hugh O'Hare had done to help quell the Great Stink had prompted the Royal Society to donate to him the old storage building in which he had developed the technology that had solved the problem. The submersible filtration drones that gathered and evaporated the densest of sewage had garnered him the acclaim and respect of London's most elite technologists, and secured a steady stream of work ever since, and ultimately the attention of the Queen and the inauguration of the Albion programme. The workshop was in sight now, surrounded by a dozen others like it which her father also owned, but this one was unique, identifiable by the water towers and weather balloons tethered to the roof on which she had played as a girl; chimneys and vents and clockwork solar dishes for converting all of nature's energy into power for the work going on within.

There were no men stationed outside, no familiar bowties or sculpted facial hair awaiting her arrival. They must be inside already. She made for the side door, slowing to make a quiet entrance.

Abigail twisted the door handle.

The noise choked instantly beneath the din of a dozen windows shattering, brickwork heaving and bursting. The discordant symphony of flame and force bathed her skin in searing heat as the workshop exploded from within.

*

Thoughts and memories coalesced and scattered like raindrops on glass. Is this what dying felt like? Life, transient and arbitrary, strobing in front of her eyes like a broken kinoscope, moving images turned to static, a flickering chiaroscuro punctuated by sounds and smells long forgotten.

She was a child, climbing the drainpipe outside her father's workshop;then she sat with her mother and learned to sew, pricking her fingers clumsily with a pristine needle. Her father gently tied beneath her chin the bow of the bonnet her mother had made her, embroidered with lilies, before he sang her a lullaby and tucked her in to sleep, promising good dreams. She was taking her first skyboat journey, clutching both her mother's hand and the railing as London shrank away below. She was on horseback, pounding across the American desert, then scrambling across Parisian rooftops as gunshots pulverised chimney stacks.

She knelt before the Queen as her first orders were given.

*

Up amongst the gushing vents and squat water tanks of the workshop roof, the air was different; something to do with the machinations within, the discharging energy and the churning water of her father's equipment. Or perhaps, had her young, eager mind been able to fully articulate the concept, it was the sense of potential, of the electrifying creative energy strobing beneath the slates and steel sheets that she had mapped in memory and could traverse with her eyes closed.

"I don't want you up there!" her mother would rebuke when she heard tales of her daughter scaling the drainage system and making a playground of the labyrinthine network of filters and reservoirs. "It's dangerous!" she would start, turning away from the fine gowns on which she worked to trawl her usual list of possible tragedies. "What if you were to fall off and break something, or get steamburned, or incinerated, or fall in a tank of rainwater and drown! What *then*?"

"Well, I'd be dead, wouldn't I?" Abigail would insist, lips pouting adorably in a face inevitably smeared with dirt and oil.

Where her mother would chastise, her father would enact what he thought was parental anger, the sort of pantomime shock he rarely dispensed, and only doing so while in ear shot of Josephine and her sewing needles. When alone with his daughter, he was likely to be found in the maze of the factory rooftop with her; it was he, in fact, who had shown her the best way to climb the walls to reach it, and they had an unspoken arrangement that Abigail would never tell, as long as she remained extra vigilant when loose up here.

It was a few days past her ninth birthday and they were up amongst the nesting pigeons, eating a picnic lunch her mother had prepared in the belief they would eat it in the workshop. She was taking tiny bites from a sandwich and tossing small chunks to the greedy birds.

"What's it to be after our feast? Mathematics?"

She wrinkled her nose, half due to his suggestion, and half from encountering a particularly tart blob of mustard within her bread.

He scowled unthreateningly. "If the home schooling is to continue, young madam, you have to do it all."

"It's boring!" she argued with the absolute certainty and honesty of youth. "I like the engineering and the physics, not the boring numbers stuff!"

"Without the digits and the division there wouldn't *be* any of the exciting stuff. How do you think I do what I do?" He waved a small apple pie at the towers and pipes around him, at the greater skyline of London across the Thames, the pistons and cogs of Tower Bridge, the steamsleds gliding the streets on cushions of compressed air, the buoyancy spires of the submersibles in the river. "How do you think we did all of that?"

"Magic," she offered, a wry smile creeping its way onto her cherubic features for the first time, and certainly not the last. "Like you told me about those men who made gold out of metal." She looked proud of herself. "Al-kemmy."

Her father took out his notepad, never far from his fingers, and leafed through the densely scrawled pages to find a blank space, and he spelled the word out for her, correcting her pronunciation.

"Alchemy is just a story. Science with your 'boring bits' removed, and you don't get far without them. What I do isn't magic, my dear. My base metals are all up here." He tapped his temple as he often did when making a point about the power of the brain. "My process is science—the equations, the numbers—and my gold is the betterment of human kind."

Her face turned up to him, red hair glowing in the high noon sun. She did not look confused, just a little lost, like a further nudge was required to tip her into understanding. Despite his passion for educating her in the facts of science, he would loathe himself entirely if he were to completely remove the notion of wonder from his treasured little girl.

Below them, a sleek steamsled arced its way through the docklands and hissed to a stop outside the workshop. Her father's whole demeanour changed, shoulders dropping, gaze darkening.

It was Mr. Belmont, one of the men who gave her father regular jobs, asked him to solve problems, and to build things for him. She heard her father talking about him with her mother sometimes, where he would become flustered, agitated and very unlike her father. It was in those conversations that she heard her parents talking about money, about stability and safety, about things called ethics and duty. Mr. Belmont made her parents feel bad sometimes, and she had come to recognise his narrow face and sunken eyes, his red bowtie and pathetic little moustache, as features of danger, not to be trusted.

Those features now stepped from the steamsled, a serving man opened the door for them, and they strode on spindly legs with overwhelming self importance up to the base of the building. The sunken eyes turned up to look at her father.

"I have no time to waste, O'Hare," he shouted impatiently.

Her father nodded, and spoke to her quietly. "I'll be back in a moment. A challenge, while I'm gone." He flicked through his notepad and retrieved a small piece of rectangular card, perfectly, pristinely white save for the seven triangular, circular and square holes punched clean through with surgical precision.

"When I return, you can tell me what this is."

He shimmed down the drainpipe to shake hands with Mr. Belmont, leaving his daughter to ponder the task.

*

With six year old eyes she marvelled at her mother and father dancing at Christmas, kissing beneath mistletoe, and she hoped to be so very much in love when she was old enough. In a crowded hall her father was honoured with a shining medal pinned to his lapel, and later she lingered by a door in his workshop she was forbidden to enter, listening to angry arguments echo from down the hall, her father telling men precisely what science made possible and precisely what it did not. She lay in the arms of a good man, a bad man, and several shades between.

She dreamed of being born.

She was.

*

Abigail breathed deep, drawing in stale oxygen. The stinging sensation in her skin did not subside until she spilled herself from the deep iron bath in which she bobbed, sprawling on the cold wet floor. Her eyes adjusted to the gloom around her, and she recognised nothing in what appeared to be a medical facility, some strange experimental bay. The bath from which she slithered was connected to a series of smoking, sizzling copper tubes, all running to quiet, squat machines dotted about the place.

Her last memories were of the skyboat, of looking out of its portholes at the star-glittering ocean a thousand feet below, of falling into the pillows of her plush cabin, of filling in her daily journal with all the vigorous detail that Archie would transform into cavalier fantasy. She had tied her bonnet to keep her hair neat and fallen into her slumber thinking of Brittania, of breakfasting with her parents and spending the afternoon in the market to replace the goggles hacked apart by the damned Cherokee.

Now she was here. There was no hum of boat pistons or the vibration of its hull. She was no longer aboard. Someone had seized her in the night, dosed her with some anaesthetic concoction, smuggled her off the craft and spirited her here.

Everything hurt, every muscle and pore. Her hair was tangled and slick with antiseptic and slurry, sharp cheeks flushed, pale, freckled flesh goose-pimpled in the chill, bringing the realisation that she was naked. Bare wet feet slapped across the floor as she searched for rags to swaddle her.

Instead she found clothes, draped on a mannequin amongst the maze of tables and dynamos; linen culottes and a white blouse, finely stitched, elegant but functional. Abigail had seen enough of her mother's handiwork to recognise it instantly. She dressed.

She felt like a hospital patient, stumbling around a ward in which she had not been properly cared for.

Something familiar caught her eye on a nearby table. It rested on a small wire sculpt of a baby's head; a lily-stitched bonnet like the one she had worn as a child, similar to the ones she had worn to sleep in ever since. Her attention was quickly drawn to a second object on the table, of far more interest and of a much more elaborate design: a series of pivoted spindles suspended over an etched plate, connected with gears and tubing to a brass funnel. It looked like what her father would produce if asked to replicate one of the stylus-voxes she had seen in the advertising sections of the paper, the sort of frippery reserved only for the self-importantly wealthy.

Her mother *and* father had been here, and she was sickened to think they were being similarly tested as she had been. There were many names that ran through her head, those she had wronged, or righted, depending on the way one assessed these situations. All of them were loose ends from old assignments she had yet to tie, or cut off.

She reached out to touch the device and heard a familiar voice behind her.

"He said it would take a year and a day," Archie said, hobbling closer on a bronze cane, perusing a quietly ticking pocket watch in his withered hand. "Right down to the second. Your father always had an impeccable sense of timing."

"You!" Abigail held out a hand to make him hold his distance. "Archie, tell me you are not responsible for this! I have enemies by the dozen and I do not think I could handle the newest of them being you."

"I am not your enemy, my dear. Just a lowly caretaker tasked with tending the O'Hare family estate, and it's most prized possessions."

"Where are my parents?" she demanded, her deep sense of violation tempered only mildly by his soothing words. "Where am I?"

"You are home, Abigail, as home as you have ever been. Follow the staircase to the top and unlock the door. You will recognise the workshop, or whatever little of it remains."

She hesitated, looking past him to the foot of a stone staircase, winding up out of sight. She thought of bolting for it, but the danger-stoked fire inside her subsided now, replaced by a wash of tentative confusion. Her quivering voice sounded childishly small. "What is happening, Archie?"

"Sit down a moment and gather your breath."

She drew up a high wooden stool and sat timidly; looking around for further signs of her parents, but found none.

"You have nothing but my deepest sympathies, my dear," Archie said, and flicked the tiny lever that set the styluses working through the imperceptible grooves on the plate and listened to the distant, scratching echo in the funnel. A familiar voice murmured from it in the darkness, small and far away.

*

At the passing of an hour Abigail O'Hare ascended the staircase and emerged through a door that had always been forbidden to her as a child. The workshop was a ruin, the early morning sun lancing through huge holes in the masonry, the mechanical evidence of her family's legacy all but destroyed by explosives. But the damage was old, the smells of chaos long since faded.

It took her little time to find a new route up to what was left of the rooftop.

The skyline had changed little, yet it seemed alien, a year and more removed from *her* London. She heard her father's words again without the need for the stylus-vox. They were rooted in memory now, planted in the fresh, fervent soil.

"My dear Abigail. I will not be there to speak face to face, and for that I send my sincerest apologies. I trust Archie has kept his word, and kept you safe. I send you this promise: nobody can hurt you now.

"Of all the people you ever dealt with, the thieves and kings and warlords, it was that cheap roustabout Belmont that figured it out and arrived with his threats and his designs on blackmail. What Albion does for Queen and country is one matter. What she would be made to do on the whims of a thug is quite another.

"In the struggle, we argued and we fought, and the workshop was reduced to ash. Your dearest mother gave herself to protect me—you always got your bravery from her. It was not until I pulled myself out that I found you outside. From me, it seems you inherited a flair for timing. I make this recording in my final hours—I was still injured in the blast and will perish soon. I exist now merely to bring you below and commence the arrangements for your care."

"Your brain was in tatters," Archie had told her in the darkness of the laboratory in which her body, barely clinging to life, had healed and gestated for many months. "You were naught but a dribbling wreck, but your father had always known how to fix you, if ever he needed to. Clever old bugger, that one."

Abigail turned the bonnet over in her hands, examined the inside, tracing the delicate lily patterns; what eyes had once seen as gold threads were now seen as intricate crystalline fibres like miniscule versions of those that powered contraptions and carried words and data to processing engines.

"When you were a little girl you had such nightmares. So we made you a special bonnet and we told you it would fill your head with such wonderful dreams. A small white lie to trick you into believing. I did not give you dreams. I merely fathomed a way to write down

your memories so, should the need ever arise, we could always make you whole again."

She examined the squat, nondescript buildings surrounding the remains of the workshop. Archie explained that her father had left everything to him, but that he would sign it back to a willing O'Hare without question. She did not know what to do with the factories – no, they were warehouses, she knew that now. Stocked with a near-infinity of small white cards, no identification but for the configuration of their punched holes. Destroying them felt petty and strangely murderous, but the notion of a blank slate was decidedly poignant in the here and now.

"You wore it, and continued to, because you thought it made every dream a delight, but every one of them -- those were all yours."

She would cry properly later for her mother and father, long since ensconced in the womb of the earth. In this moment she cried only for the gift she had been given.

"When Britannia called, you served. You never questioned, and for that we were ever so proud, but with service there was never a choice. That was always my goal. To give you that choice. Britannia thinks you're dead now. A year will have turned when you look upon London again. She may need you now more than ever, or she may have learned to stand on her own. But what matters is that the choice is yours now, and yours alone.

"My time grows short. Just know this. Though we were told to raise the daughter of an empire, that never meant that we did not raise our own."

With the faint warmth of the morning sun on her cheeks, wet with tears, her mind, brand new and as old as ever went back, to a memory that was vivid as the day it was made

*

Her father returned to find her sitting cross-legged, examining the white card with its many shaped holes. He seemed happier now that Belmont's steamsled was leaving the docklands.

"Well?" he asked.

"I know your lessons," she said sternly, having rumbled his intent. "*This* is the mathematics, isn't it?"

He beamed, clapping his hands together once with vigour. "My dear, the complexity of that mind of yours scares me sometimes. A million of those cards could barely contain its knowledge."

A familiar air horn blasted half a mile away, and her father consulted his pocket watch. "Right on time," he said excitedly. "Watch this. Look."

He lured a pigeon closer with a scrap of bread, and gently enclosed his hands around it with minimum struggle. It cooed as Abigail brushed her fingers across its ruffled breast, pecking her gently. Her father gripped the tip of its wing and spread it fully, revealing shimmering feathers of purple and green.

"This beautiful bird never asked to fly. How could it?

It cannot speak, or even truly think as we do, and yet she was granted the most wonderful means to soar above the land. How is that fair?"

"It's not!"

He passed the bird to her and she held it with gentle firmness, running her thumbs up its warm back as he retrieved the card.

"The way these cards are cut, the way they are sequenced and processed by the calculating engines, they turn the unfairness of nature into a very human possibility. We worked out scientifically what made the fishes swim and we cut the cards..." He pointed out at the river and spoke in an urgent, excited whisper, "And we cleaned the Thames! We calculated the power of the horse and we built the steamsleds."

Abigail smiled with uncontained glee, eyes wide and hopeful; she had worked out what her father was doing, but loved his theatrics. Whatever he might say, she *knew* there was magic in him. She was already getting to her feet before he urged her to, hands gripping her shoulders to ensure she remained facing the river.

"And," he whispered over the noise of the approaching spectacle, the din of clanking ratchets and hissing, evaporated liquid. "We fathomed the very numbers of the pigeon's wing *and...*" He shouted to be heard, waistcoat tails flapping in the wall of hot wind that rushed up at them from behind, *"as if by magic, we learned to fly!"*

She knew what he said, but the final words were all but

lost as the skyboat soared above them, barely a hundred feet away, the gleaming steel and copper of its hull reflecting sunlight and bathing them in its radiance. Its stabilising wings unfurled on their slender, skeletal rods, set in stark relief against the balloons above, coruscating with fizzing blue light, and the swirling gas lighter than air itself. Exhaust pipes like cannons on ancient sea ships released columns of steam to steer the gliding airship on a true course, veering left now to sail towards the river, out to the sea and away on its journey to exotic climes.

Abigail tossed the pigeon skyward. It was momentarily battered and confused by the wake of the passing ship, shedding feathers in the hot, spinning air, then righted itself and flapped off over London.

Abigail grinned as wide as Hugh O'Hare had ever seen. "Let's do the mathematics, then!" she beamed. "But *only* if I get to fly one day!"

"Oh, you will," he insisted. "I have no doubt of that."

*

The truth of a nation rests in its people.

As she wandered the avenues in the marketplace, taking in its delights, its smells, the richness of Britannia's tapestry, she still felt its vibrancy, its life. Little had truly changed in a year. The past was merely yesterday.

Of all the familiar sights, one roused her more than any other, made hear heart and mind soar with the same joy it always had.

The children were playing Albion.

COGS

I'd let you cut me open,
  see what it all looks like inside.
The clockwork heart,
  the cogs that don't quite tick right.
Climb inside and tinker,
  teach me to keep time again.

THE HIT

She hobbled my heart, my capacity to care.
Splintered my passion until the marrow wept out.
She was hammer and blade,
  a glamorous sociopath,
  with a surgeon's precision,
  and the loving smile of
  the best of friends.

COLLECTION

I collect
  your sighs and screams,
  pleading, pleasing mewls,
  and the yowling, shuddering cries
  to a deity that ignores
  the likes of us.
Your breathless whimpers,
  bratty rebellions,
  thank yous served alongside
  satisfied tears.
I file them neatly in a
  quiet chamber,
  play them again
  one by one
  to remember and
  all at once
  forget.

PRISONER

I'm imprisoned in a cage of your making.
My crime is loving you.
My three square meals a day are
  your smile;
  your heartbeat;
  your caress.

DAYS

There are days
  of deviant and dark desire;
  frivolity and fun;
  of dolorous doubt;
  passion and play;
  deft defeats and roaring success.

They are you,
  all those days.

SHAPES

What shape would our lives be
   had we only met sooner,
   capable of a unity that
   would shatter our worlds
   for the better?

Somewhere we're strangers,
   and somewhere
   we're lovers.

Here is the melancholy joy
   of the somewhere in between.

PURE HEART

She dreams,
  of only sweet things;
  fairytale endings;
  boundless poetry;
  magical creatures;
  hope where there is none;
  and fucks that last forever.

WASTE

To the days I've wasted,
  the seconds sent to slaughter:
  you're remembered as
  potential unfulfilled
  in a graveyard
  strewn with could-have-beens.

LONGING

I long for yesterday's touch,
  for kisses now forgotten,
  for dreams that didn't die,
  and laughter that lingered.
They're faded now,
  bleached by a cruel sun,
  living eternally
  on the tip of the tongue.

BECAUSE

I write because I cannot paint,
  or conjure music sweet.

I write to let the demons out,
  in the hope they will be beat.

THE PARLIAMENT OF EMILY

A single tap cracks the old mirror into a webbed map of fractures, tines of weakness waiting to fail. Each facet reflects an off-kilter shard of who she is, a hundred familiar eyes behind each of which lie a hundred unfamiliar memories. They're there, waiting for her, and following in time. She inhales hope and exhales fear.

They all count to three, and it echoes into the forever of potential. Every voice is hers, but the tone varies, or the timbre, or the accent. Some whimper, others declare, others huff and puff and blow all doubt away.

Emily taps the epicentre again, and the slivers of her rain down, leaving only the frame. She tumbles through it as if gravity flows on the horizontal axis. They're all falling in circles. Leaves in a gale. Fabric billows and hair tousles. They always land on their feet in the glade's familiar ground.

This is how they meet. The Emilys.

They come, one by one, until they are a multitude, filling the forest with their laughter, their questions, their perfumes and their unified heartbeats. Spiralling rings of them stretch away to the horizon, but each is heard with crystal clarity without the need to shout, even though they all talk at once. That is their connection; the same fundamental materials, identical clay shaped by differing hands. Each has walked a divergent path based on choices and circumstance. Left or right. Heels or flats. Fight or flight.

It is impossible, but they make it work.

"It's good to see you all," Emily smiles, and feels love, hatred, union, bitterness, friendship, kindness and despair all at once. Not directed towards her, or any of this strange sisterhood, but residing in a hundred hearts. Some come broken and bruised; others triumphant, glowing with their euphoria. There's indifference, sarcasm and bliss. There are those who tell of their children, and those who never ventured down that road. There are those who found love, and those who have stopped looking entirely. There are the athletes and the bookworms, the lean and the large. There are the ones who teeter on the verge of giving up and the ones who never could. There's an Emily with the bandages at her wrists covering fresh scars laced across ones that healed long ago. She confides in an Emily who never made the second set of cuts, and then in a pair that never made the first. Emily who lost her left leg below the knee after a car crash, jokes with Emily who runs three marathons a year, and all the while her heart aches to run again. The drinkers call the tee-totallers prudes, the non-smokers berate those who do. The businesswomen envy the hipsters' freedom, and the slackers envy the go-getters' drive; some will see a template to strive for, and others will never change their ways.

They've all vowed, and then truly learned, not to judge. Each is the current progress of an infinite cascade. They're water rushing across jagged rocks. Some are swept along down channels, some choose which to flow down. Some made choices others never got. Others ignored opportunities that never came again. It is infinite, unpredictable, and unquestionably fair. They all see their lot, where they might have gone, and where they might go still.

They all know they are the lucky ones, because some don't come at all.

Even though the absent aren't there to tell their tales, they hear them. The frame spills the secrets of the fallen, echoes from paths that came to an end. There are ballads of those felled by freak accidents, and of those not strong enough to continue. One Emily was taken by an aneurysm, a bomb in her brain she was never once aware of, even when it exploded. Another was hit by a drunk driver and perished in a coma a week later, never given a chance to say goodbye. Another still had her light extinguished by one who claimed to love her, pleading with bulging eyes until his wicked hands completed their ghoulish deed.

And there are the Emilys – too countless to calculate – who suffered the same diagnosis too late. Some fought hard, some railed and withered to bitter ends, some made peace and succumbed with love ripe in their hearts, unquelled by the blossoming darkness inside. Of the Emilys here and now, there are those who won't meet here again. And there are others who will fight and win.

Emily hopes she will be one of the winners, and believes it. She doesn't resent or envy the ones who have not suffered. It's not their fault. She draws from them the strength that she can, takes inspiration from the could-have-been and never-was. She takes comfort that she's not the only one going through this, every time she comes. She consoles and inspires those who have it worse, and shines her warmth like the sun.

Before they all leave, she holds an Emily close who never lost her hair; she smells it, holds her palm against the back of her head as this Emily whispers her goodbyes, and she looks forward to the moment when hers begins to grow back.

They fall through the frame in reverse, storm-tossed motes in the eddies of forever. They land back upon their own paths, bolstered to keep walking, a step at a time.

Emily looks into the mirror, and Emily looks back, the one she is used to seeing every day. The Emily who made her own choices, dealt with the ones that weren't hers to make, and continues to forge ahead. She strokes her bald head and puts on her fedora, because it makes her look cool, and paints her smiling lips the colour of fire. It helps to burn away the pain and doubt. She blows herselves a kiss.

The old glass hangs in its gilded frame, scuffed but unbroken.

She likes that.

MEAL

I'd eat your pain, swallow it down.
I'd let it rot me from the inside out
  if it meant you
  could bloom.

TOUCH

"Touch," said the temptress. "Take me."

The very air was basted
  in her musk and perfume.
She radiated sensation and fire;
  the cold could not penetrate her.

So I would.

CURVES

You have the kind of curves
  I love to get lost in.
Great heaving swells of flesh,
  vast valleys of pink delight.
My love for your shape is as
  hefty, buxom and warm.

THUNDER

Loving you is to court thunder,
  to kiss rain, dance with lightning.
You're nature's crescendo,
  and I'm tossed within that
  glorious storm.

FIXATION

She obsesses on the oral;
  the rims of wine glasses
  her tongue caressed;
  the cigarettes and
  dicks she sucked;
  the lip-chewing notions
  she's considered;
  the baby teeth the
  dentist pulled.
The stolen kisses,
  pouts and spit;
  girls she's licked;
  all the swallowed pride; the
  sores and scabs and salves;
  escaped secrets
  that should have stayed
  inside.

<u>THESE HANDS</u>

These hands.
They've fondled flesh and dreams,
  caressed your hair
  and slipped inside your intimate secrets.
They've soothed, slapped,
  squeezed, scratched,
  secured.
They've flexed around
  and fingered
  every inch of
  willing skin.
They enveloped yours
  to give them
  strength anew.

WORDS

I need the words.
They're medicine,
  the most bitter,
  palatable pills,
  swallowed and spat out
  to ease the ills.

ILLUSION

The grand illusion,
  the showstopper, the act.
Pretending we're okay.
That those wheels are secure, that
  the rules are there for our safety.
That the void isn't whispering
  the sweetest nothings
  into an ear too willing
  to hear them.

TO MYSELF

I just hope it gives
  some illusion of coherence,
  some semblance of sentiment.
I'll type volumes
  with only thumbnails and half smiles
  to show for it.
I rarely read it aloud,
  like they say you should.
Reading it aloud makes it real.
It makes you feel.
And that's always the first shot.
The salvo of warning.
So I keep it to myself.

ARTWORK

You don't belong on
  wall or plinth.
You're tactile,
  to be savoured
  with every sense,
  painted for private study
  sculpted for scrutiny.

ALWAYS

You will always be,
  without regret,
  whom I was most proud
  to let into my life to
  make the place
  your home.

UNITY

I know it as soon as the door clicks closed behind me; I am a fly in the spider's web. I'm not even sure how you did it without me seeing you; you slipped into the space behind me and pulled the blindfold across my eyes, fastened it with nimble, firm fingers. I saw nothing but the descending veil of darkness, but every sense now heightens to accommodate the one that has been suddenly starved. I can smell you like a banquet, heady and rich and intoxicating. I'm glad I can no longer see, for I know I would be dizzied by that scent.

Your breath on my neck galvanises every hair to stand, a parade of scintillated threads on an ocean of rippling gooseflesh. The shiver sweeps through me like a wave, every cell in my body part of an eager crowd throwing its hands in the air in exultation. The sounds you make are a symphony; the intake and exhalation of sweet air, the satisfied moans as you examine every inch of me; and the sound of your voice as you tell me that tonight, as forever, I am yours.

Then your touch… It's like being caressed by feathers and hit by a train all at once, every pore and muscle reacting to your eager, capable fingers. You combine gentle care with powerful precision, a well-oiled construct designed for my pleasure. Hands sweep down my spine and dip across my buttocks, swooping across my thighs and up over the swell of my chest. You've explored this canvas a thousand times before but each time feels like the first. Your expertise is bolstered by experience but you make it fresh at every turn. I crave that touch like an addict, and when it comes, I never want it to end for fear of crushing withdrawals.

I am in your thrall and at your mercy, devoted and locked in servitude. I always have been, since that very first moment; this is merely a physical manifestation of every inner thought and sensation I've experienced since you bewitched me. Even when *I'm* in charge, as you lay at my feet and do everything I command, the control is always yours.

Your swift digits find the clasps and buttons of my clothing and pick them apart, one by one. You guide me to step from my shoes, my ankles breathing a sigh of relief after such a long day, and I can think of no better cure for stress than you. My clothing falls away piece by piece until I am naked but for the fabric barring my vision. I shiver in the warmth of the room, every pore and nerve alert to your beautiful game.

You guide me to the bed and lay me out, sprawled, spread and secured with bonds I still cannot see. My ankles and wrists are wrapped, my limbs straining playfully; the steel frame of the headboard and bedposts whine gently but offer no quarter. I am here for as long as you enslave me; I hope it is forever.

Naked beneath you I succumb to your power; it manifests through fingertips and lips, skating across the surface of me, but also in the complete and utter control I surrender, as I know you'd surrender it to me. Your seduction is total, through action, word and the unbroken devotion you show. I'd do anything for you, and I'm sure, before the night is through, I will. Your tongue pours its love upon my most intimate of areas and I'm beholden to its every flick and expert ministration, moaning with each deft, darting touch. You assure me I am yours, and I have been no more certain of a single thing before in my life, and I will be certain of it forever more.

Arms enfold me and entwine, and our nethers merge, drawing satisfied breaths from lungs that bellow in perfect unity. Desire lubricates the piston-precise motion of undulation, gliding like angelic machines built solely for this purpose. The tension at our loins surges amongst a miasma of thrusting, sweat, saliva and shared lust that divides like cells, spreading through us, a perfect viral flood of endorphins, sizzling nerves and orgasmic glee.

We climax together, the opening salvo in a war of bodies and minds that will rage all night, and I shall surrender in every battle and allow myself to be stormed, invaded and seized.

You take off the blindfold and I see you in all your glory. The beauty of you is blinding, but I have looked upon you so often that I am almost resistant, like I've stared at the majesty of the sun long enough to see it truly. You look upon me the same way, and my heart aches, because I can never truly put into words the complex yet simple perfection that is being allowed to love you.

GENTLEMAN

I don't want to be the gentleman.
I want to be the wild man.
The animal.
The big bad wolf who
  huffs, and
  puffs, and
  blows your mind away.

THAT MOUTH

That mouth of yours…
I love the way it curls up at the corners,
  the way it whispers secrets,
  the way it hungrily opens wide and
  how it swears and howls for more.

THRALL

I see a girl who may blush
  at a bad word said in public,
  but one who turns to an
eager wet thrall
when the same word is
growled in her ear.

ABSTRACT

I love watching you apply
  your makeup.
The plush
  gloss of lipstick,
  dark strokes of mascara.
I love it most for
  I know, later, I will
  smear it to streaks.
I'll make of that
  beautiful portrait
  an abstract mess.

ADORED

He adored:
How she danced
  with two left feet
  and spanked his ass
  when he shaved.
The manner of her melancholy
  at the happiest of songs,
  her joyful tears at birthing sunrises.
The way she sucked him
  with her eyes closed,
  breathed his name on
  contact with coming.
That she tasted of
  cherry liquorice, and
  smelled like promise and need.
How she thought he was funny
  when he knew he was not,
  and let him believe
  he was right.
He adored:
Her.

HURT

I want to hurt you,
  in all the ways you crave.
Leave on your body
  marks that will heal.
Make you shed
  tears that replenish.
But the scars I'll leave
  in your heart and soul
  will never fade.
They'll be your most
  cherished wounds.

HUNGER

I hunger.
I'll devour you.
Every morsel.
Every quivering sliver
  a succulent treat.
Every sweet inch
  a delicious buffet
  of willing flesh.

NOCTURNAL

Noxious, nocturnal,
  she wears the night
  like high heels,
  breathes darkness
  in sighs,
  prowling for
  black thrills
  to kill the
  need inside.

DROUGHT

Their speed was legendary and she used it to tease him, vaporising like mist and coalescing several feet away; each time she reappeared she was in a new state of undress, and sometimes she would put an item back on to impress. Each fleeting portrait of her was bookended with the whoosh of oxygen rushing to fill the space she had been, gusts of perfumed air spinning a dizzying tornado around him. He whirled to keep up with her. She moved across his vision like a scratch on his sclera, a beautiful eye worm that flitted to and fro each time his eyes shifted, ever elusive until she was upon him, bounding off the floor and wrapping her legs around him, locking tight. His back hit the wall and a poorly rendered landscape painting hit the floor.

To his eyes she was clear as day, to his body as weighty and solid, but to the mirror she was a ghost. In its frame, his body writhed with a pair of nylon holdups wrapped around his waist, stuffed with air the shape of her exquisite legs; a corset hovered and flexed against him, the interior cups filled out with the shape of invisible breasts; light reflected off everything she wore but passed right through her flesh. His senses gave him shades of the truth, his peripheral contradicting that which was before him. He didn't care to fathom the illusory realities.

Her tongue was a dervish in his mouth, her sharp nails knives to a silk shirt, rending from the collar and arcing down his back. She swallowed the hiss he made as the tattered strips of expensive fabric flew in braids and draped the cheap furniture. He became aware that he had never been holding her when she clinched his wrists and slammed them either side of his head, and still remained perfectly balanced against him. She supported herself with the strength of her thighs, but gravity was not entirely an enemy to her kind; they could somewhat break its bonds, resist its pull. She hovered at his abdomen, the heat of her sex radiant against the rampant bulge in his slacks.

The maiden leaned away to gaze upon him, mouth hanging open, revealing her teeth, exposing the myth of fangs as fabrication. Her teeth were perfectly white and smooth, no tapered incisors in sight. She inhaled through her mouth, then her sweet nose, drawing from him what she craved the most, that which ensured her survival, the invisible breaths and testosterone-tinted aura pouring from him. The flesh above her cleavage flushed red swiftly, ignited by the hit of her addiction. Her eyes shifted, kaleidoscoping into snowflakes around pin-pricks of onyx; his scent was in her, the energy of him pouring, mercurial and electrified. He was her battery.

She pivoted back, palms hitting the carpet, legs releasing, flipping up and over. She cartwheeled in a blur to the bed, already in a crouch, ass thrust towards him, her sweet crevices bare of threads, glistening for him. He threw himself to his knees, hauled down by an invisible but unbreakable chain, crawling like a dehydrated fool to a desert oasis, and without a beat of hesitation buried his lips into the succulent buffet of sin. She pushed back to meet him, merged his lips with hers. He burrowed his tongue into her hot sliver, suckling her with unbridled joy.

The physical pleasure of it was a thrill to her, but it was dwarfed by that which she took from him; the physical tremulous sensations that bristled were secondary to the orgasmic warmth that spread through every vein, fibre, atom. His desire for her was the thing that sated her beyond any physicality; he craved thismore than anything, and that was the energy she took from him. It invigorated and enriched and bought her one more day. His tongue slithered across her offerings, lavishing her with saliva and pulsing pressure. He gulped and nibbled and drooled, and between her buttocks felt arousal like he'd never had before. She took it all.

She sensed his desire was shifting focus to his engorged groin. She flickered like candlelight and used superior strength to lift him, rolled him onto the bed where she wrenched his trousers down and off in a single sweep. He barely had time to register his stiff prick hit the air before it was at the back of her throat. Her hands guided his own to her hair; he balled it into fists and his hips bucked, involuntarily only for the first thrust. The rest were intentional and fevered, deep and aggressive. She widened her throat to allow deeper plunges, until her mascara surged in faint rivers down her hollowing cheeks.

He pulled her off him at last. She sucked in lungfuls of air and his flowing aura; to her it came off him in ribbons of gaseous colour, rainbows of glee crystallised into the visible spectrum. They cascaded from his sweating skin and crashed against hers, burrowing beneath the surface until she glowed from within, a radiance he was as incapable of seeing as he was her reflected flesh. She inhaled it, bathed in it, absorbed its every speck. He saw none of it, but the texture and tone of it shifted as his hunger hankered for a new sensation.

In the blink of an eye she straddled him, lowering onto the swollen totem, directing it with giddy hands to the tighter hole he had eaten so heartily. It swallowed him, resistance fading with each new inserted inch until her buttocks distended his thighs. He filled her so completely. His quivering hands came to her braced knees and squeezed with every bounce of her. She was a fevered animal, working a pendulous, pornographic rhythm.

With each thrust he poured dancing torrents of colour

into her. Her sliver trickled desire and he danced his fingers through her moisture, licking his fingertips. The musk hit his tongue and morphed into spirals of opalescent gossamer. Fractals of intangible coral coruscated back into her; her skin drank them, her soul enriched, her hunger reaching the point of satisfaction. She needed now the explosion and worked for it, rocking, frictionless around his girth. The bedsprings cried for mercy but were drowned beneath his cries of climax.

The spectrum merged around them, torrents of crimson, ochre, jade and violet cast backwards through the prism until they coalesced into blinding white. As within her he gushed and coated, the rays of white lanced out, hit the walls of the cheap hotel room, ricocheting in shattering shards that span straight back to her, kissing her body like a beautiful blizzard and melting to darkness. The lightshow blinded her for a string of blissful moments, her senses whitewashed into delightful, momentary death.

She slipped off him. It was too dark for her to see it, and she felt it only distantly, the way one feels something as anaesthetic kicks in; his seed trickling from her and staining the sheets amongst their sweat. He gasped and panted beside her, drained of desire, and colour. She felt like the proverbial fortune, bereft of shame; that, she left to him, to writhe and wallow with.

His passion was stolen now. He would no longer find solace in writhing roughly, in lapping at nature's tinctures, in thrusting. It would be perfunctory, joyless, and soon given up, like an old bad habit.

With a flurry of motion she dressed, pressed a sweet kiss to his cheek and stole into the night. She took with her the vibrancy from within him, desire sucked dry to sustain her own soul, leaving the silenced stranger alone, forever, in a colourless world.

BLEED

Creativity seeped
  from veins to
  pool at feet,
  the last remnants
  manifesting as
  shreds of verse;
  anything more
  fled in the bleed.

COMFORT

My hands find
  comfort on flesh,
  solace on skin, a
  perfect purpose
  when there's
  pressure applied.

READ MY LIPS

Slick with temptation and
  needing elation.
Glossed and primed for
  luscious suction and
  plush eruptions.

Read my lips.

WETTER

It's better wetter.
The drenched clench
  of thighs wringing,
  sighs singing.
Muscles clamp
  on fabric damp.
The fervent gush,
  rich and lush.

SWEAT

The heat is oppressive, and we're driven inside seeking the solace of shade. In the stifling atmosphere of the kitchen you pour yourself a glass of water, sip the icy nectar to slake your thirst, but I have other plans.

My shadow casts on the wall as I approach; you are dwarfed, and have no time to prepare. I press against you, the bare, moist musculature of my chest against your back, my arms enfolding you, guiding the tumbler away from your lips and angling it with care. You anticipate the splash of mercurial water across your neck, your bikini-clad breasts, but it's still a surprise when it comes.

You yelp.

*

You slip your finger into my open mouth and I close my plush lips around it, sucking, tasting the salt of your sweat, and your hands cup my breasts, tracing through the rivulets of water that washed away the natural gloss my pores provided. The cleanse will not last, for nature has shown her fiery mood today, and my own body responds in kind to your touch.

I *want* to sweat for you, to slip against you like oil, skate across your skin. I grind the cheeks of my buttocks at your shorts and feel you, all ready for me; you watched me bask in the glow of the sun and could not contain yourself. I know it's all for me, and it makes it all the more a delight to feel.

Your tongue trails my shoulder, leaving a wet wake through the droplets on my flesh, and you end the trail on my neck with a sharp nip and a lingering kiss.

Take me.

*

The ropes of your hair drape between my fingers as I clench my hand and tilt your head back, savouring the gasp you release. I empty the last of the glass across your chest and imagine the water hisses as it hits the sun-heated floor. That is the last thing on my mind now; you are at the fore, your taste and your scent, the wetness of your skin against mine.

My finger tips dive the plunge of your stomach to the

cove below, seeking the hidden treasure nestled between quivering thighs, peeling back the covering and cresting the moistening rise of your desire for me. You let me in and I find your most intimate pearl already waiting for attention. Your texture and your mewls strengthen the length that needs release.

I walk you to the couch and tip you across it, pinning you with my weight, the oily canvases of our bodies unified and one.

*

You are sensual, beautiful and caring so often, but I love when you are like this; animalistic and desperate. This is raw and right. I seethe as you arrive within my being, filling me so ably.

Your sweat splashes my spine and you steel yourself with my sodden locks. My flesh weeps with heat and exertion and you lap the tangy tincture away in slaloms of sensation. There's silence but for the sound of wet flesh slapping and our primal, ragged breaths.

I tighten inexorably around you and I'm blinded by the heat of the moment when I howl my desire.

*

You shudder beneath me, every muscle twitching under your glistening bronze skin. You bury your face to mute the sound of your abandon and I feel you explode with divine familiarity.

I spill within you; a floodgate unhinged, pouring every drop in a torrent of intimate intrusion. We're doused and drenched, saturated and stuck to one another by biology and lust. I cling to you as the final clammy inches of skin seal together. We're a cocktail, mixed and blended, inseparable and complete.

The dew cools but the heat remains, and I kiss the red welt I nipped on your neck, and forever refuse to peel myself away from you.

INTOXICANTS

Be my whiskey shot
   and my cigarette.
I'll binge on
   your intoxicants and
   worship the hangover.

SLIVER

There's still a sliver of you
   nestled inside,
   the thorn that burrowed
   all the way,
   a stabbing reminder
   of regret.

INNOCENT

Innocent is a distant shore,
  of a forgotten land
  unsullied by time.
Setting sail from its
  hopeful sands
  is to say
  farewell forever.

BROKEN

We're all of us that
  little bit broken;
  bruises, fractures, sprains.
Scuffed and bandaged daily,
  scar tissue in place
  of brains.

TREAT

She thought there would be nobody in, but as they stumbled out of cold into the narrow hallway, Erin could hear the others. Music from the living room up ahead, all bass and pounding drums, made the mirror on the passage wall vibrate with a rhythm that beat in opposition to her heart, still thundering after the flight through the rain. Adrenaline crawled back into its hiding places, and she balked at how much the E's thrall still held her. Her tongue stuck to the roof of her mouth.

"Drink?" she asked the murderer.

"Anything."

She gripped the transparent plastic poncho that covered him, blood staining her hands, red, pink, purple and brown and everywhere in between. She led him towards the room where shadows of a party played on the walls, avoiding her reflection in the hall mirror, refusing to stare into the bloodshot pits of her eyes. Her back teeth ground within a tightened jaw.

The murderer examined himself in the mirror, and through his narcissism, she saw him now as if for the first time. Hair slick with cheap product and more blood. Ice-scuffed black shoes a size too big. The cheap suit he'd told her he wore for work, wherever that had been, looked loose on him. The axe was in his frozen hand, still matted with the tangled hair of a fresh kill. He was taller and thinner than she remembered, mere shades from skeletal.

In the living room the TV was on, music playing through the speakers, the warping, psychedelic rainbow of a games console's CD player undulating in time with the beat. A thin veil of smoke hung around the yellowing paper lampshade. The incongruity of the mismatched furniture struck her for the first time since she had lived there: a leather sofa and upholstered chairs, and an old tartan deckchair. Crushed cans and empty bottles lay where they had fallen. The gig-night posters on the walls, ripped from chip shop windows a thousand late nights ago, were muted, the colour as drained from them as it was from her cheeks.

Four others gave them cursory glances, barely rousted from their revelry. A cross-dresser in a blue wig and fishnets, pouring a glass of white wine for a large bald man sporting a backpack and William Wallace face paint, who was expertly rolling a joint; Elvis Presley, spread on the laminate flooring, head in the lap of Pippi Longstocking.

His eyelids drifted, barely awake, idly playing with a red pigtail as she gently stroked his chest.

"Check out the murderer," the man in the skirt said, and thrust out a hand with cobalt painted fingertips.

Erin's high-heeled leather boots clacked the floor, barely audible over the music. In the adjoining door-less kitchen she took two beers from the fridge. She noticed the ladders in her black stockings, the tear in her corset, exposing the cups of a black bra. The curves of her breasts and pale throat were flecked with red spots. She wet some kitchen towel and wiped herself clean, wondering where the eye patch had gone. Without it she looked like a mere harlot. Cold moisture dripped onto her exposed shoulders; her hair still bore the last remnants of raindrops.

The murderer took a swallow of his beer, watching her carefully. She sipped her own, awkwardly avoiding his gaze.

"Thought you were out all night?" Erin wondered aloud to her roommates.

William Wallace snorted. "Jam packed. Bunch of pricks dressed like twats. Present company excluded."

"How was Jonesy's party?" Pippi asked, fingertips brushing The King's neck as his eyes grew heavier. "Looks like you had a good time."

The effect of the weather on her cheeks, coupled with the confusion of the last twenty minutes, hid her flush of embarrassment. She offered her guest a wry smile, then took the gentleman murderer's hand and led him from the room, up the stairs fitted with an old, ugly carpet, past a door with a biohazard sign and into a small bedroom that smelled of josticks, perfume and old weed.

She sat the murderer down on her bed. He perused the gallery of photographs around the vanity mirror above the desk; Erin herself, family and friends, a beloved pet, single instances transformed to moods and feelings, memories replaced by images. She turned on the CD player, an inoffensive female voice singing gently from the meagre speakers, unable to mask the noise of heavy bass from the room below.

"What are we going to do?"

"Don't worry," he said, and he went to put an arm around her.

Then she looked at him, solemn, and all the colour seemed to have gone from his eyes. What she recalled from the first party as being a captivating green were now slate grey, uncertain and unreadable. Her icy fingers clasped the back of his neck then and brought his face close to hers, lips meeting forcefully. He tasted cold, of vodka and saliva and of her own cherry lip balm. The kiss spoke nothing of desire, but desperation; she hadn't wanted to cry, for her lips to quiver, so she kept them occupied. Her stomach lurched as her hands tore clean through the flimsy rain protector draped over him and snaked between two buttons of his shirt, cold hands rolling across the raised xylophone of his ribs.

At times it felt like she was viewing from a distance,

watching herself tug off his trousers, as if seeing a flawless lookalike doing it on television. At others she was amongst it and he was too close, breathing and sweating on her. That was the ecstasy working its way out of her system, throwing her in and out of the fray. The encounter was swift and grasping, punctuated by the dull pain of colliding shoulder blades, climaxing with gritted teeth. Cheeks pressed together, he held his face in the pillow as she looked at the ceiling, trying desperately to think of nothing, but incapable of thinking of anything but the grim reality of what had happened tonight.

She clasped his hips and slid him from the only warmth her body was capable of. Her quivering hands reached for a cigarette and she lit it clumsily, dropping it to leave a tiny brown-rimmed hole in her bed sheets. It was then the first tears came, falling silently. Words creaked from her dehydrated lips.

"We have to go back."

She threw on crumpled clothes from a heap on the floor and he put his suit back on, and the poncho, carrying the axe with him, the blade now a rusty brown. They went back out into the night, followed the route back to the park without speaking, her mind racing with possibilities and no solutions. On any other night they may have looked out of place, but a giggling zombie, a staggering nurse and a Batman pulling on a hip flask passed them and didn't look twice. It was the simple matter of time and geography that had spared that revelling trio the same experience had by the axe murderer and the pirate wench. Had Erin insisted on a different route, or had she pulled him from that party any earlier or later, then those three could have been here now, incapable of rationalising what had befallen them, whilst Erin and her new companion could be oblivious and happy, grinding and gasping in each others' arms.

She hated the park without daylight. The vibrancy given to it by laughing children, barking dogs, and students playing football, all evaporated when darkness fell, creating a hostile and frightening wilderness, where every shadow held a secret menace.

They found the ruins at the same spot they had stood for hundreds of years, squatting in the tangled mess of shrubs and weeds, incongruous opposite the darkened bowls pavilion and children's play area. A faded circular plaque bolted to the ancient brickwork gave a dry history of what the place had once been, but she had never cared to read it, and couldn't focus on now if she had wanted to. The structure was now merely three and a half towering walls thrust towards the sky, roofless, gazing at the stars, an obsolete reminder of a time when the laws of men were different and it was so much easier to bury a mistake.

"What are we going to do?" she asked, a question aimed not just at the immediacy of their situation, but stretching off to encompass an uncertain future. "We could go to the police, tell them what – "

"No," he cut her off coldly. "It doesn't matter what we tell them."

He kicked through weeds still bent from their last passing an hour ago. Moonlight reflected on slivers of long grass where the blood was still drying.

Erin sniffed behind him, imagining her world crumbling away like the remnants of the building, a life of potential reduced to dust and ash. Every second of it now had been wasted. All that time spent on frivolous nonsense, in studying things she didn't understand, sleeping with people whose names she'd never remember. Taking substances designed to make her stories more interesting, defiant for defiance's sake. Smoking to poison slowly the body God had given her, only for him to walk out on her now, slamming life's door in her face without even the need to say 'I warned you' or 'I told you so.'

The murderer called her name and she followed him, hesitating in the narrow archway leading into the closed border of looming rock. She heard him laughing uncertainly, and knew why before she checked for herself; this night had gone so fiercely off the rails that anything after the initial blow was fair game. Absurdity didn't matter anymore. It was the norm in a world where she was witness to murder, and had tried frenziedly, pathetically, to cover it up.

The body was gone.

They had left him slumped in a corner, propped up, in ragged clothes that reaked of his urine, cheap cider and countless nights living rough; anybody who found him could assume he had sat there of his own volition, huddled against the cold October night only to lose a battle with the elements and expire. Harder to reconcile with that picture was the gaping cleft in his skull, splitting skin and bone from his left eye, across the forehead to the wild hairline. Half of his bearded face had been soaked in crimson, a nose painted with broken veins plotting the course of alcohol-thinned blood down onto a weather-beaten shirt and coat.

Now the corner was as unoccupied as it had been for a century, but the evidence was still there. The stone where the vagrant's corpse had lain was soaked darker in places, the thick of it having run off down cracks in the stonework, the old soil beneath drinking in the spilled blood.

Erin's voice quivered, unable to function properly amidst the heady mix of flooding relief and frightened uncertainty. "Where is he?"

"He wasn't dead," the murderer stated. "We didn't – "

"*You* didn't," she insisted sharply, unsure of why she was still trying to clear herself of something that perhaps had not happened. If it had, it was an act not performed by her own shaking hands. It had been *his* hand on the axe, felling a man who didn't even have time to look confused about the rusty steel wedge that bifurcated his eyeball and lodged itself in the delicate grey organ behind it. Her involvement was simply in watching a homeless man die, a man whom had harassed her in a drunken stupor. She hadn't expected her new suitor, in his fake-blood-streaked poncho to do anything aside from shove the tramp away.

He had swung the hatchet without her say so.

Before this horror, at Jonesy's party, he explained to her why he carried a real one; a last resort because he had no time to buy a plastic alternative. The toy and joke shops were crammed to bursting with those who had left the festivities too late. The one he had in the yard at home had fallen to ruin along with the saw he had used to break down the cheap wooden frame of an old sofa, but it would serve the purpose just as well. Once the initial showing off of his costume was complete, he had discarded it in a corner and devoted all his attention to her. As she led him to the door with silent promises of her naked body pressed against his once they reached her own place, she remind him he had left it. Erin's only crime tonight had been common courtesy.

"It must have just been shock," he said calmly, hovering by the empty, bloodstained stone. "People survive head injuries all the time."

"But if he's just wandering out there, he could get hurt. He's blind in one eye! He could step in front of a car."

"Then he's someone else's problem. Not ours. Look, someone will take him to the hospital. He'll be fine." He rushed to her, grabbed her upper arms tightly. She writhed to get free of his grasp. "We're okay, we got away with it."

"*You* got away with it," she insisted again, twisting free, utterly repelled by him. She needed a shower, to cleanse herself of him; everywhere he had touched and licked felt tainted, and she spat any last traces of him onto the cracked stone.

Her stomach convulsed. She vomited. The murderer reached out again to try and help her.

"You stay away from me," she rasped, wiping her lips. "You did this. This was all you. Just stay away."

She fled, leaving him standing in the ruins. He didn't shout to stop her, and he didn't pursue. It was starting to rain again now, stinging her face as she sprinted back to the flat. She stumbled through the living room where Elvis Presley snored alone, almost tripping over him in her rush to get to the bathroom adjoining the kitchen. The shower head sputtered and steam flooded the tiny room as she stood beneath the jets, scrubbing her pale skin raw. Later she dragged herself on weak legs up the stairs, pulling all her weight up the handrail, shuffling past the door with a biohazard sign, beyond which she heard a vocal Pippi Longstocking sharing her body with the blue-rinsed transvestite. In the silence of her own room she tore off the sheets soaked in the smell and stains of shame, and fell onto the unmade bed, where the needs of her body took over, pulling her eyelids closed and shutting down her brain, leaving it working just enough to give her dreams of twitching fingers clawing at ancient masonry, and blood soaking into earth.

*

The murderer went home to his flat to find the corpse

sprawled on his couch, watching a late night television station where women in lingerie writhed and moaned and pretended to answer phone calls.

The blood on its forehead was dry now, and it wore the pirate wench's discarded eye patch over the ruined orb, the remnants of which had congealed in the ginger, bloody bristles of its beard.

"Very funny," the murderer said, his breath misting in the air. The things presence had dropped the temperature several degrees. "We're finished now, you can go."

"Just making the most of the facilities. You seen this?" it gestured at the television, then at its groin. "Nothing. I haven't had a rod since I died. The time I died for *real*. Blood's like dust. This is just raspberry sauce." It stroked its beard with atrophied fingers.

The murderer dropped the hatchet onto the coffee table and took off his poncho, bundled the crinkling plastic and shoved it in the bin. "Go. You're done."

"I forgot how tame this was," the corpse continued, ignoring its host, eyes transfixed on the TV, on a willowy blonde unfastening her bra. "I die in three years time. They go all the way by then, whether you call in or not. Guess morals start to slip."

"So you came back in time for me?" the murderer yawned. "I'm honoured."

"Time doesn't mean much of anything when you're dead. That sorry cage we call skin and bone can only go in one direction, but all that soul and essence gubbins, that's free to go wherever it wants."

"Out."

The corpse released a sigh, a breathless vestigial gesture. Bones creaked and disintegrated, muscles stretched and snapped as the corpse hauled itself upright and put its meagre weight on kneecaps powdered by decay. The murderer watched it lurch a few steps, barely able stay on its feet. How this pathetic bum had been able to put on the show he had paid so much for, he couldn't fathom.

"So she went for it?" the corpse wondered, smelling of damp and rot.

"Touch and go for a while. You never know if they're going to freak out and run screaming. But usually all that fear and confusion, they just fall into your arms."

"Was she worth it?"

"Every penny."

The corpse grunted. "You're going to hell, you know that, don't you?"

"See you when I get there. Now piss off."

The corpse showed a smile of blackened teeth and peeled off the eye patch caked in sclera, pushing it into the murderer's palm. It laughed.

"Be seeing you."

The corpse was there, grinning mockingly in his face, and then it was gone, in the time it took him to blink. The murderer stood alone in his small flat with only the noise of a plastic rain sheet unfurling in the corner, and the faint bass of another Halloween party in the flat below.

He showered, the water close to boiling but unable to warm him. The icy aura leftover by the dead man's presence just wouldn't lift. He toweled off, wrapped it round his waist, and padded to the kitchen, inspecting a fridge devoid of anything to eat, but the chilled air inside was the warmest thing in the whole flat. He poured a large measure of whiskey and drank it in one, feeling nothing but discomfort as it burned its way down his gullet. No warmth. He poured another and sat at the computer.

He logged into the website which he had first disregarded as a joke. The idea of it had stuck with him until he jabbed in his credit card details and had proved the theory that it really was possible to find *anything* on the internet. Mail order brides were one thing, escorts and slaves and those eager to be eaten for sexual thrills were another, but the rental of the willing dead for whatever purpose the paying client could devise was its own thing entirely.

Precisely *how* it worked, the site was vague about, and he didn't really care how they ran the operation, as long as it ran smoothly. He paid his money, a servant from beyond the grave turned up in the flat to take orders, and a terrified and bewildered girl submitted to him. It was that fear that made all the difference in the intimate encounter; he'd charmed enough damaged souls to become addicted to the thrill of fear. A woman in an abusive relationship, a girl facing trouble with the law; not knowing when the axe would fall was a powerful aphrodisiac. He had sought to bring that to its extremes, and had swung that dreadful axe himself.

Every damned penny.

He filled in a customer feedback form, indicating his general satisfaction with the service, but adding a complaint about the quality of the agent they had sent. Not his appearance – after all, it wasn't his fault he died of hypothermia in clothes that smelled of stale urine – but his general attitude had been poor, and he had left the place freezing cold. If it was still that way in the morning, he would be asking for a refund, or at least a discount off his next transaction.

He knocked back the last of his whiskey and stumbled into the kitchen to pour another, not noticing the axe on the coffee table was gone.

The lights went off. The computer cut out, the fan whirring down into silence, and the naked girl on the TV turned to a shrinking point of light and faded into nothing. In the flat below, the bass continued. He muttered his misfortune and went fumbling for the fuse box, nestled into a cabinet at the top of the stairs that led down to the front door. As he reached, the towel fell round his ankles and he laughed at how stupid he must look, naked and grasping in the dark.

He felt the icy palm in the small of his back too late, and the gentle shove was enough to tip him off balance and cast him down the stairs.

Impact with the skirting board shaved off the cartilage

of his nose. Ribs shattered, pushing through goosepimpled skin. Patches of flesh grazed off against the wiry carpet. A link in his spine leapt an inch to the right. His neck jarred, head taking the weight of his body as it hit the scattered array of unopened junk mail and pizza menus on the doormat.

He couldn't move, or breathe properly, or cry out, naked and helpless. The party next door continued, the din of his fall masked by the rhythm of their music. His moist eyes flicked around dumbly, then rested on the landing at the top of the stairs.

Erin was watching him. Her hair was wet, hanging in snaking tendrils across her bare shoulders and naked breasts which he had cupped and kissed so little time ago. Her thin hips swayed as she descended a few steps. She didn't look cold, and no breath condensed as it left her lips. There were marks on her wrist, vertical slashes between the sinew, precise cuts that would have poured life into a hot bath in no time at all.

She put the bloody axe into his open, twitching palm and sat down gently. She watched him without saying a word, sat like that all night, never moving, never blinking.

The murderer was just as incapable of closing his eyes, of seeing anything but her, across those endless hours stretching out to dawn. The door to the neighbouring flat opened and closed a dozen times, potential rescuers passing inches from him. He could not rant, or rave, or seek help or forgiveness or absolution, as blood slowly flooded his lungs and stomach, poisoning and choking him until his eyes saw their last: the spectre of a girl who would soon wake up to a world that she no longer trusted, living bound in a needless guilt that would drive her, over weeks, to madness, with an insidious fear that only a blade could quell.

Satisfied, Erin rose, aware of the one-eyed tramp behind her on the stairs, warmed by his presence, vindicated, hopeful, and yet utterly empty.

"How was that?" she asked.

He laughed, the sound of slaughtered dreams.

"Welcome to the team."

ALL THE LADIES WANTED

Suzie craved an audience
  on binary streams made wetter.
Money helped essentials,
  attention true was better.

Emma wanted reassurance
  that the bullies weren't correct.
Traded exposed pictures
  for those of souls erect.

Donna wanted three men
  to disregard her honour.
To forget she's half a daughter,
  and pour their seed upon her.

Maria wanted kisses
  down below til dawn.
Better than the ones he gave
  with half a heart through yawns.

Hannah feared prudishness,
  so set an endless goal.
To fuck a league of brothers
  to make herself feel whole.

Kathryn hated being betrayed
  by promises of truth.
Met a man in leather gloves,
  lived at last a misspent youth

Debbie took on boredom
  with whips and chains and toys.
Had her husband trussed and owned
  by neighbouring girls and boys.

Collette had no grievances
  just a desire to perform.
Signed a willing contract
  became a fleeting queen of porn.

Annie wanted pets
  beyond the pure domestic.
Had specks around the globe
  obey her rule majestic.

Sally needed stuffing
  a cure for all her ills.
Sought to be packed tighter
  until everything was filled.

All the ladies wanted
  to know some kind of care.
For some migrant moments,
  assurance that they're there.

<u>AFTER</u>

Betrayal's cold glacier
  carves a broken bond.
Shores of spite
  bite shameful seas.

Whispers to another
  flutter dead photos.
Promises now pox
  on a toxic breeze.

Trust ignites,
  passion erodes,
Loving vistas
  reduced to ash.

Silence sobs as
  fertility fades.
A wan sun weeps for
  fidelity's crash.

LESSONS

She learned to love from soap operas,
  was taught to fuck by porn.
She longs for worlds of romance books,
  and dreams of being reborn.

FEEL

Feel the poetry kiss and kill,
  taste the words as they slice and spill.

Hear the hopes, the wary dreams.
  watch the heart burst at the seams.

SHATTER

Without you
  I'd be in pieces.
But some dark days
  I dream of
  what it would be to
  shatter into shards,
  beyond repair.

AGONY

Agony
  at your side
  beats the
  anaesthetic
  of life
  without
  you.

I TAKE

I take her
    when she prettifies her perfection,
    over the nightstand,
    reflected animals
    playing at manners.

I take her
    when she showers, or I shower,
    and we've come to do
    private things,
    so we dirty and clean
    ourselves anew.

I take her when she rolls smoke
    from supple lips,
    off an acid tongue,
    addicted to the heady fumes
    of her poison.

I take her
  in the car, her mouth controlling
  speed and drive,
  hands on gears, and I take her
  in the back seat, in the front,
  in wooded groves and parks of cars
  where strangers see
  in shameless droves.

I take her
  online when she asks,
  a shrouded face and body posed,
  and I take her when they say
  they love her
  but never like I do.

I take her
  in fear
  of taking her no more.
I take her in the dark when she's scared,
  in daylight when she dreams,
  and in all the shadows in between.
I take her when I hate her,
  when I love so hard it burns.
I take her everywhere, for she took me
  long ago in turn.

A TOAST

Here's to the dirty,
  here's to the damned.
Raise a glass to the twisted
  with deviant hands.
A toast to the warped
  and the constant cravers.
To the willing surrendered
  and the dark enslavers.

DO THINGS

Do things with me,
 twisted things
 that affirm we're nothing
 but base desires
 dressed in flesh.
Let go of rules and limits.
We'll find deep extremes of
 submission and release,
 lofty taboos to
 smash and raze, and
 new delicious darkness
 in our primal hearts.

HARDER

"Harder…" she begged

"Harder," she demanded.

"Harder…" she expected.

"Harder!" she commanded.

INSTRUCTION

Take me, own me,
  bend me, brand me.

Choke me, slap me,
  never unhand me.

THROUGH WITH GENTLE

I'm through with gentle, and done with soft.
I want to hoist your flesh aloft,
  by the hair and watch you squeal,
  part your thighs and delve to feel
  the dew brought on by playing rough, then
  bind in chains and slap on cuffs.
Take your throat without remorse,
  make mascara drip and course.
Gasping, gagging, made to weep,
  moisture pools, desire seeps
  from every tantalizing pore
  as you sob and beg for more.

GLOVED

Encased in leather,
  each finger walks the length of her.
The gloves are tainted.
They've soaked up her sweat;
  touched falling tears,
  strained in a cracked throat;
  been scuffed and sanctified
  with clamping teeth.
She has branded them
  as they've bruised her soul.
She's in their fabric,
  interwoven skeins,
  strengthening with her
  gushing, pouring essentials.
They apply tasteful torque
  upon her tongue,
  digits delving,
  at their most tender
  and most violate.
Armoured by her.

WELCOME HOME

I know you are waiting for me as commanded when I enter the house and the door clicks shut in the silence; I can smell your perfume, delicate, sweet citrus, and I follow the trail you have left me. Each step I take up the wooden staircase echoes throughout our home. I am slow and deliberate, each step mirroring the rhythm of my heartbeat. I cannot yet hear yours but I know it thunders quicker with each encroaching stride.

My feet find the plush silence of our bedroom carpet and I linger there, listening for your breath. It's slight, distant, but I hear it as clear as if it were gasping in my ear. Soon, it will be. You await in silent expectation, and I can deny myself the sight of you no longer.

In I step to find you kneeling before me at the bedside,

your hands dutifully clasped behind your back, and, as mandated, you are bare. Every inch of skin is flush with gooseflesh, and the swell of your breasts become points aroused with chill and longing. Your eyes widen with excitement, servitude and desire, and my heart and body swells at such a real reaction.

I am what you want. In the mirror that stands at the foot of the bed we are a vision; you, pristine and naked to your core. I in my charcoal grey suit and silk tie, my coat still hanging from my shoulders, my collar upturned against the elements outside. I flex my fingers in the black leather driving gloves and the material creaks. I play a digit down your cheek to your chin and turn your face up towards me; I watch those pupils dilate within their glittering irises and it thrills me to see how much you crave what is to come.

You will not speak, but there are no such caveats for me. I smile. "Good girl. Now let's begin."

With a slow movement I unzip my trousers and slip my leathered fingers within; I watch your eyes follow the motions with care, and you bite your plush lower lip in anticipation. I unleash myself, threading it into view, the only exposed part of me but for a face wearing a mask of pride and expectation. Your eyes drift back to mine, and you angle your head to stroke the white cliffs of your cheeks against my engorged flesh. You gently move your jaw so I can hear the moisture within your mouth, and your hot, quivering breath shimmers against my skin.

I place my gloves atop your hair and slide them slowly

down to your temples, tickling the flesh of your ears as I put on pressure to remind you of your role. You never disobey, and your mouth widens and approaches.

"That's it," I say. "Nice and slow."

I pull you onto me but I can feel you moving despite my insistence, devouring every rigid inch of me slowly, hungrily, right to the root. Your eyes bulge and prickle with tears but you will not tarry or shy away from the duties you so adore to perform. It's your fantasy and mine, entwined as one, as soon shall be our bodies.

I am lost within you, every sense I have heightened and primed by your performance. I delight at the sounds you make, like you're savouring the most delicious meal you've ever tasted. It honours, humbles and arouses in equal measure.

"You're a goddess," I insist, and your eyelashes flutter with humility. "Now, climb onto the bed."

With saliva glistening upon your lips and chin you stand without ever breaking the clasp of your hands at the small of your back, and I guide you into the position I crave. Your buttocks sway and I marvel at the curve of your spine in the mirror, watch musculature undulate as you lower your face to the sheets. One gloved hand crosses both of your wrists and holds them tight in the small of your back, as the other runs from the nape of your neck and rings vertebrae, hurdling my restraining arm and coming to rest at the crest of your pristine valley. I delve to the twinkling, dewy furrow, and even the slightest touch with one finger makes you quiver and gasp.

"Are you ready?" I say coolly.

Your coo of agreement is the only signal I need.

I push inside slowly, steadily, my knuckles passing your lips with ease and you gasp out in glee. I move my digits rhythmically, flexing them back and forth like a swimmer's legs, caressing. Every inch they emerge shows them slick. I adore the way you squall and shudder at my touch, the way you thrust back gently to meet me. It makes my primed muscle ache for you, and as it glistens with your spit it's almost as if it twitches towards your radiating heat, desperate to plunge into that sweet canal my fingers tend.

I put a glove to the back of your neck and hold your face to the cool white sheets, bearing down with pressure to arc your back and allow my fingers deeper. Your fists ball in the small of your back and you gasp. I recognise the encroach of your orgasm; it is as familiar to me as my own. I know every inch of you. Where to touch. Where to apply that extra attention.

I hook my fingers down and tug with a rapid, fierce motion, and the reaction is instant; you moan, low and guttural and desperate, and as the pads of my fingers find your most delicate of spots your body quakes. I know what is to come and I relish the sight; you flood and spill, delicious splashes of your sweet nectar founting from you and running down glistening thighs. The first day we discovered you were capable of this was revelation, and I adore bringing you to this wet climax as much as you do. I direct my throbbing member into the path of the spray, coating myself in your celebratory champagne. My fingers slip free and the last of your tincture drips in rivulets down thighs and across the crooks of your knees.

"Very good girl," I say. "You make me so proud."

You are not quite cogent yet, words and logic lost in the orgasmic miasma. I need no further invitation than your raised, presented buttocks. You weep for my arrival and I can deny you nor I the pleasure any longer. Wet gloves grip tender cheeks and I need to do nothing but move my hips until I hit that sweet target.

I plunge deep in one swift motion. You cries are unrestrained, your body roiling, and when it appears you will break the self-maintained clasp of your wrists I close my fingers to keep it steady. It gives me leverage and I thrust using your own body to lever myself to your core. You are white-hot and wholesome, searing me with your inner fire. Though you are prostrate for me now, it is I forever in worship of you.

I gain speed, pounding without mercy. The love we make is beautiful, but that is for another day; this is raw and brutal and necessary. I keep my breathing measured, my motions fluid, but the animal within me is pawing at its chain.

I cannot, and will not, fight to contain it anymore.

I take a handful of your hair and wrench you back and off the bed. A gloved hand squeezes your breasts and elicits strident yelps, then clutches your throat to catch the sounds before they can fully escape. My other hand dives between your thighs and finds your tender trigger, circling and strumming.

You are trapped within my folded arms and with each thrust you are lifted slightly off the bed. You are weightless when you are here, invisible to gravity and bound to no anchor but me. You know not to articulate words but your moans and squeals and gasps are a language in which I am fluent. You crave *my* words now, to bring you to your exquisite end.

I bite your earlobe a moment then growl in a tone that slays your senses: "You are beautiful. You are perfect. You are mine."

You are no longer present. My words carry you across the threshold into bliss. Your physical, flapping body is restrained within my hold, but your mind is elsewhere, cannoned from this plane. I am soon to follow. The pulsing, squeezing , tightening of your pelvic muscles, and the cascade of gushing joy that flows from you and across my trousers, is my own trigger.

I expel my passion inside you, crystalline liquid that coats, fills and overflows, backwashed in your own desire. Our cocktail rains upon the sheets, a stain that will wash out, but the way we have marked each other's souls will never fade. It is indelible, forever.

I breathe and rasp into your ear, and you go limp in my arms, a fluttering leaf on a turbulent wind returning to earth. I cradle you, soothing you with gently-stroking palms. You are relaxing totally, dwelling in a satisfied haze.

You are safe, protected, and you shall forever belong to me.

"I am so proud of you," I whisper. "Always."

WHEN THE WAR ENDED

When the war ended
  he surveyed her.
Her cheeks a massacre of
  mascara and tears,
  mouth agape,
  a quiver of smears.
Her throat a scornful
  red haze, breasts
  at the crest of
  roughhoused desire.
Her body a road map
  of brutal whims
  and desperate,
  essential needs,
  bent, bruised with bliss,
  dripping in glistening sin.
Her core, open, weeping,
  spilling her secret spoils,
  and the mercy he granted.
Her mind,
  a battlefield silenced,
  suspended in peaceful,
  perfect glory.
She had
  surrendered for now.

VELLUM

Vellum lips part,
  anticipating artistry.

His tongue writes poetry
  on her.

His rhyme is her reason,
  his oration her elation.

Words awash in her
  cascading cadence.

Parchment welcomes dripped ink,
  a new verse complete.

She is made of his masterpieces.

FOLK

There are these folk,
  they hang
  on my mind's street corners
  where it's always night,
  where all the avenues
  named after my mistakes
  converge.
They dress like
  gentlemen, princesses,
  criminals and whores.
Their horns and tails
  poke as they
  whisper and jeer,
  plotting dark deeds,
  drinking and smoking
  and teasing,
  sucking down addictions,
  sullying the clean,
  fucking fearful strangers
  under neon signs that
  sting eyes to
  slow blindness.

SUPERSEDING TREVOR

It usually took a respectable average of four pints of Old Speckled Hen, and a shot or two of something Scottish and amber, for Trevor Trent to tell his 'I met a superhero once' story. Decidedly less if he started imbibing on an empty stomach, as had been the case today. Usually it was just his well-worn attack in the battle of verbal one-upmanship, deployed when he needed to swoop in and rightly declare himself the conversational victor, but today it was primed for a different purpose: to impress a girl.

His colleagues were as pleasantly tipsy as he was. The day's deadlines, crunches and targets were behind them. It was Friday, and post-work drinks were brushed with a veneer of relief and hopeful excitement for a weekend that would go by too fast and yield little in the way of creative or personal growth. All six of them crowded round a too-small table in the nearest watering hole to their building, ties loosened, high heels kicked off, breathing in the sweat and smug success of a day of good solid graft.

In the world of estate agencies, Sterling Residential was, by a small margin, at the top of the heap. Not the kind of long-hours, nose to the grindstone job that would leave you sleeping three hours a night with nothing but a worn, bloody strip hanging in the centre of your face, but neither a slacking, laissez-faire operation that dealt only with poor students and pensioners. Their customers were comfortable and middle class, their properties equally so, their sales techniques tailored accordingly. The firm owner, Dexter Bleak, presently slurping the head from his third Guinness, liked his employees to pursue all opportunities with a persevering tenacity, eager yet never overt. But Dex also liked to shut up the office early on a weekend to beat the rest of the local businesses into the Dog & Parrot. Trevor had once joked that Sterling Residential was like *Glengarry Glen Ross* with less swearing and a better social life. His peers had laughed at that, all but Suzy, who'd never seen *Glengarry Glen Ross*, a factor that Trevor had deemed to be a great shame. He still intended to lend it to her on DVD, but suspected it would go unwatched among a stack of chick flicks and *Gossip Girl* box-sets.

Suzy Sanderson had worked with them only a few weeks. Dex had chosen to ignore an empty CV in favour of an ample cleavage, and a penchant for short skirts. She was always cheerful and bubbly, with the kind of smile you couldn't hold a grudge against for long, regardless of how limited her viewing habits were. Though she had not, to Trevor's knowledge, been intimate with any of the men in the office, she had a whispered reputation of being, in Dexter's unprofessional parlance, 'a bit of a bike'. It was an accusation based on nothing other than her dress sense and an apparent lack of much between the ears. With a sliver of shame, it was she that Trevor was saving his prized story for.

Joining Trevor, Dexter and Suzy at their cramped table were The Twins; James Johnson and Kenneth Spericki were neither brothers nor bore any likeness to one another, except for a vague similarity in height. They'd simply walked through the door one after the other one unremarkable day and Dexter had greeted them with the nickname that had stuck for so many tenuous years. If boiled down to online profile-friendly soundbites, Jimmy liked cars, James Bond and Steve Perry-era Journey; Kenny was into cricket, curry and Queen. Trevor liked them well enough to share a few laughs over drinks, but was quietly glad their time together went no further than a post-work pint.

Capping off their sextet – or the Property Patrol, as the Twins had named them all during a bored afternoon – was Pamela Preston. She was their diligent accountant, the only one of their number who held down a marriage, a family and a healthy lifestyle, throughout a rich life which, had the gentlemen in the office been true gentlemen, they would never have guessed totalled a wrinkle-defying forty five years. Trevor liked Pamela the most amongst his workmates. She was warm, charming and caring, could keep pace on a night's drinking and knew more dirty jokes than the rest of them combined. Being twenty years his senior also made her strangely protective of Trevor, a maternal affection that he pretended to be playfully scornful of but secretly liked. Nothing cloying, just a genuine interest in his wellbeing.

Dexter was finishing his oft-heard saga of the time he met 'that bird off of that programme that isn't on anymore' to the customary faux applause and snide remarks about the encounter's veracity. Before Jimmy or Kenny could begin a tale of their own, Trevor slammed down a half-empty pint glass with enough force to slop it all over his wrist. He ignored it and ploughed on, drawing a deep breath.

"Here he goes," Kenneth muttered, and Trevor pretended not to hear it.

"With what?" Suzy asked.

"The 'I met a superhero once' story," Dexter yawned.

"You met a superhero?" Suzy repeated, without sarcasm.

"I met a superhero," Trevor announced, eyebrow raised dramatically.

The other men leaned back, allowing him the floor but ready to snipe throughout. Trevor rarely enjoyed the thrill of this, hating how transparent it was. He saw everyone around that table with a Y chromosome, every penis-toting simpleton as a simplified bald peacock, unable to show their feathers so opting instead for the muscular or vocal equivalent. Trevor had never been a strong man, no matter how many attempts he had made at the gym, but he liked to think he could tell a story. He leaned in closer to lay down said story as thickly as he could.

"It was a dark and stormy night!" Kenny announced theatrically.

"It was indeed a dark and stormy night, Kenneth," Trevor agreed without stumbling, cursing his companion with a sharp glance.

"There was a chill in the air and fear on the streets, remember," added Jimmy, stuffing peanuts into his mouth and pretending not to stare at Suzy's cleavage as she reached for her wine glass.

"It was very chilly, and the streets were very fearful, thank you James. By the way, you've got a salty mess on your chin." He shot a quick glance at Pam.

"Not for the first time, either!" she cackled, to raucous approval.

"It's the end of a long hard day, and I've worked late to carry out an audit, or whatever bullshit Dex had me doing that night."

A chorus of 'oohs' and a mock-offended face from the boss pierced his words.

"I'll do my own punctuation, people. My car's in the garage and I have to bus it home. I'm walking the last few hundred yards, and I cut down an alleyway, and suddenly..."

He let his voice trail off to silence, to let Suzy lean in closer.

Jimmy whispered: "Milk it, son, milk it for all it's worth."

"There's a guy running towards me at top speed, he's carrying a purse. We're nowhere near the Pink Triangle so I doubt it's his. And I see a body slumped down the alley. An old woman. She's unconscious."

"He'd mugged her!" Suzy offered.

"Nothing gets past this one," noted Pam, into the echoing acoustics of her glass.

"And this guy's running at me," Trevor continued. "Headlong. I'm thinking 'What do I do, what do I do? Do I tackle him, do I trip him over?' I'm about to take him down when there's a shadow on the ground between us, I hear something flapping in the wind and then he's gone. Just gone. I'm looking all over but he's not there."

"Who was it?" Suzy wondered. "Who got him?"

"I go running over to the old woman, she's got a graze on her head, she's knocked out, so I try to bring her round."

"Kiss of life," Dexter chipped in. "Loves the crumblies, our Trev."

"And before she can," Trevor went on, "He's there, scooping her up in his arms."

"Captain Courage?" Suzy blurted out hopefully.

"No." Trevor tried to disguise the sound of his

windless sails withering. "Macro Man!"

Suzy's disappointment would have been audible three continents away, super-hearing or not. "Oh! That's... pretty good."

"You should have seen him!" Trevor went on, trying too late to salvage the spectacle. "The cape, the boots, the spit curl, he was amazing. He thanked me for my help, then..." Trevor made a whooshing sound and thrust his fist towards the ceiling. "He took off into the sky with her."

Suzy nodded, expecting more.

"And she was never seen again!" Jimmy joked.

Kenneth snorted a laugh. "Macro Man's probably still got her chained up in his cellar. He's a wrong 'un, that one."

"My sister saw Captain Courage once," Suzy said, changing the subject deftly without actually changing it. "It was when he caught that fighter jet at the air show before it went into the crowd. Said he flew over her head with the plane still on his shoulders like it was a backpack."

While Dexter, Kenny and Jimmy acted like that was the most significant achievement since Pasteur's bin scrapings, Trevor sat back, story ignored, vicarious triumph unsung, social victory a resounding failure.

Pam patted him on the shoulder.

"I know I don't count, but I like that story," she assured him.

Suzy took her cigarettes from her handbag. "I need some fresh air."

He thought for a second about going with them; he'd pretended to be a smoker in the past in order to prolong the company of an attractive girl, but it was a ruse that rarely yielded anything other than a sore throat the next day. The three other men escorted her outside, the four of them smoking beyond the window as Trevor pretended not to watch the game continue. Seeing it through glass made it all the more obvious and sickening, like he was at the zoo, or seeing three savages dancing around a totem pole, a pillar of sexual wonder he was destined not to climb. He cursed himself for making the scenario sound grander than it was; one of them out there was probably getting laid tonight and he wasn't. End of.

Pam dropped a fresh pint in front of him and caught him watching the show.

"You don't seriously like her, do you?"

"Of course not," he said, entirely truthfully. "But it'd be nice not to go home alone for once, even if it is with someone who's been nailed more times than a faulty floorboard."

"Look at the clip of her. She's riddled." Pam's tone softened. "That's no way to get over her."

"It's how she got over me. She got a head start too, I've got to catch up."

Trevor had avoided thinking about Natalie for all of four minutes; the last instance had been the spur to tell the Macro Man story, a pathetic attempt to secure a night of forgettable, shameful passion he'd regret the very moment it was over. His and Nat's relationship had been an eight month stretch that threw up memories ranging from intense lust and hopeless love, through to meandering complacency, past crawling suspicion to gut-punching disappointment and betrayal.

They had met, as most seemed to, when they were drunk and barely able to hear one another over the din of dreadful music. A clumsy fumble on the dancefloor led to an exchange of numbers, and a real first date that revealed they did have a couple of things in common, enough at least to warrant another few meetings. The term 'whirlwind relationship' was one Trevor had always despised because he'd never had one, but Natalie had been his own tornado, coming into his life without warning, moving all the furniture and leaving a wake of shattered everything. She had moved in to his flat too soon, marked it with the scent of her perfume, and within weeks she was heralding the whole thing as a mistake, expressing regret by sleeping with a guy she worked with weeks before she had the courtesy to tell Trevor. This, of course, she did without words. One evening he had come home to an empty flat that bore very little trace that she had ever been there. The only evidence to suggest that he had ever cohabited, however briefly, was a black skirt that, when questioned about over the phone, he swore he couldn't find, and an umbrella she hadn't cared enough to ask for.

The five weeks between then and this moment was an unsuccessful trawl for empty physical closeness, a time when his games console had seen far more action than his crotch. Still, his gamerscore had never looked healthier, something that filled him with both pride and personal ignominy.

He realised Pam was talking, and he hadn't heard a word.

"Sorry, what?"

"Doing anything nice tomorrow?"

He wasn't, and he knew Pam knew he wasn't, but a torrent of self-pity and the resulting maternal hug wouldn't have made him feel any better.

"Oh, packed schedule," he yawned. "The world is my lobster."

"Lucky you. We're taking the kids swimming, then to Nitro Bites for tea. I hate it in there, it's so tacky." Pam wrinkled her nose. "Everyone in there over ten is just miserable, especially the waiters. The costumes are so crap. I bet a theme restaurant isn't what Captain Courage or Macro Man had in mind when they started. If I was wearing a cape, things would be different."

Pamela didn't like the supers. Never had.

Trevor smiled. "I was going to fly. I had it all figured out."

Everybody, save perhaps Pam, had the same fantasy. In another life, you might have wanted to be a rock star or a Hollywood icon, but those were old dreams for an older generation. The masses wanted powers, cursing those lucky enough to have been granted them, be it by evolution or industrial accident, as was so en vogue these days. X-ray vision was the new rich, invisibility the new famous. The supers were the pinnacle of fantasy, their life of danger and derring-do synonymous with sex, style and glamour. Trevor had spent hours as a kid designing his costume, a blue one-piece with a hood and a green cape. The joy that was puberty held the promise of abilities yet-to-manifest, and even though there was no super blood in his family, he knew he'd be different.

Just like his friends at school knew. His cousins and neighbours. Looking up to the sky, knowing they were destined to soar higher and further than everyone around them. Everyone was going to be unique, and they all wound up the same. Now they all had lives, husbands and wives, rent and mortgage payments, homes that wouldn't heat themselves. Childhood desires gave way to boring responsibilities, and the world turned as it always did. Few flew. Fewer soared.

They finished their drinks. Trevor looked over at the television, at the rolling news report. Girlfight had just stopped a bunch of masked men robbing a bank, and took off into the evening sky as police loaded the criminals into the van.

Trevor pulled on his coat. "Better go, that ready meal isn't going to cook itself."

They headed outside as Dexter, Jimmy, Kenny and Suzy were crushing cigarette butts beneath their feet.

"You off?" Kenny wondered obviously and without

concern.

"Watch out for muggers," Suzy giggled, and Jimmy slapped her on the shoulder, laughing too forcefully. For a fleeting second, Trevor hoped it would be Jimmy who got lucky tonight, and hoped he was thoroughly unsatisfying.

"Or at least a decent cape," he guffawed, stumbling back into the pub with the others, leaving Dexter to wish them a good weekend and a see-you-Monday.

Trevor walked Pamela to her car.

"You want a lift?" she asked.

"I'm alright, I'll walk." His tone was enough to let her know he preferred to make the journey alone.

"I know a few girls, I can set you up if you'd like? Mind you, they're a bit classier than the Peroxide Avenger there, so I don't know how keen you'd be."

"I've never liked you, Pam," he smiled.

She kissed him on the cheek.

"Have a good one."

He watched her pull away, talking on her mobile phone, no doubt informing her husband that she was on her way, cementing plans for their weekend. The first drops of rain from the black evening sky dripped down his neck. He took Natalie's umbrella from his pocket and opened it, thankful for the meagre shelter as he trudged off down the road.

He chose the route through the burn, down old steps choked with branches and nettles, stinging his ankles. The alcohol in his system was sufficient that he barely noticed their barbs. This was a shortcut known only to true locals and drunks; Trevor was happy to be both, and the footbridge over the river would have him home swiftly. The odds of running into anyone down here, let alone trouble, were slim.

The noise of the distant traffic and pubs faded to nothing as he went deeper into the dark, the way lit by old fashioned street lamps barely cutting through the descending fog. He thought about stuffing in his earbuds and taking the opportunity to catch up on one of a dozen albums he hadn't listened to properly, but he preferred the quiet, the sound of a city falling asleep.

He thought about Natalie, about what she would be doing at that moment, likely grinding against a stranger far more handsome than he, and was glad he had deleted her number from his phone.

He thought about the misfire his story had been. What made meeting Macro Man pathetic in comparison to Captain Courage? The only decent answer he could conjure was the fickle nature of the public. Sometimes an unlucky cape just fell out of favour for no reason more complicated than the public likes a whipping boy, or girl. Maybe the cat jumped out of the tree before he got there. Maybe her skirt was hiked too high and a schoolyard full of kids went home with a few uncomfortable questions about anatomy. Them's, as they say, the breaks.

He'd thought about lying, about telling the story with Cap in place of Macro Man, or stretching as far as The

Shimmer, or even Girlfight, but what would ultimately be the point? Oversaturation was the problem. Seeing one in person didn't matter. There were so many of them around, and so many cameras and twenty four hour coverage of everything, that being all over the papers and on all channels every waking hour had lost them their sheen.

"You saw a superhero in person? I saw Manhammer stop that building from falling."

Of course you did. Everybody in the world saw that, from seven angles and in slow motion, on their Facebook page and on their phone. Seeing a super meant that you had eyes and the ability to focus them. Some power that was.

He thought about Natalie again. The caring, sweet Natalie with whom he had fallen in love, and the selfish, flighty Natalie who had broken his heart. He was unable to separate the two. He wished he hadn't deleted her number.

The rain had stopped by the time he reached the footbridge and he packed away the umbrella as he crossed to the centre, leaning against the railing beneath a lone orange lamp, looking down into the rushing water below. The fog was thick enough that he could see nothing beyond ten feet in any direction, and neither shore. There was just him in the whole world then, safe in an amber bubble, time trickling away beneath him.

He smelled cigarette smoke on the breeze, head snapping to the right to see he wasn't as alone as he had thought. He hadn't heard anyone approach, but there she was – there *she* was – smoke and hot breath drifting before her in the crisp air, staring into the water with piercing blue eyes, looking out from behind the red mask glued to her face. Her white jumpsuit looked like little more than cotton this close up, and bore dirt stains and spots of blood, and a few singed bullet holes revealing skin beneath. Her sturdy red boots were scuffed, the crimson cape hanging to her waist slightly torn. Her delicate yet powerful features were framed with a thick bob of golden hair that looked strong enough to repel bullets, and probably was, but which now hung somewhat dishevelled.

Before she tucked the pack into her utility belt, she offered him a smoke.

"I don't," he managed.

"I wouldn't if I wasn't invincible," she informed him. Her voice was like his favourite song on a warm summer evening, if that was possible, and these days, what wasn't? Yet it was also quiet, vulnerable, and tired. "And only in costume," she added nervously. "I don't like people to know."

Trevor wasn't sure how that made any sense; a crafty smoke in costume caught on camera was enough to get the ire of the public. HydroGal had taken months of flack because the paparazzi caught her with a hipflask.

He looked around for support, half expecting to see a camera crew filming his bewildered reaction, but there was nobody. Just the two of them, alone but for the sound of the water.

"Screw it, I'll have one."

He lit the cigarette, barely able to taste it, which he was thankful for.

"What's your name?" she asked him.

"Trevor. What's yours?"

"Girlfight."

Trevor tried not to cough. "I knew that."

"I'd tell you my real name. I wouldn't even have to kill you. It's just a bit boring." She hesitated a moment. "Alison."

"That's not boring."

He studied her profile, the plush pout of her lips and curve of her jaw. He knew she was beautiful, but without the mask she would have been stunning, that soft, girl-next-door type of beautiful that trumped all others. Natalie had never quite had that quality; she was very pretty but worked for it, hair and make up as contrived as her attitude.

"I heard people rarely ever come through here," she said softly.

"I know. I live nearby."

"It's nice."

She dropped the last of her cigarette into the cold water and he followed suit, thankful he didn't have to finish it to the filter. He couldn't think of anything to say. Everything sounded pathetic in his head. How did you ask a superhero if they'd had a good day, or what they were doing this weekend? He had so many questions and couldn't think of a single one. Anything he felt awkward saying to a regular girl, he'd feel infinitely more so saying to a super.

"You shouldn't feel so nervous," she assured him.

"Can you read my mind?"

She shook her head.

"Good. Not that I was thinking anything I didn't want you to hear."

She asked him where he worked, and he told her, making it sound far duller than he intended. He quickly added the *Glengarry Glen Ross* comparison to spice up the description, knowing it was pointless.

"Sounds nice," she said. "I love that film. Amazing dialogue." Trevor was quietly impressed and stole another glance at her. She added: "You can ask me, I don't mind."

"Are you sure you can't read my mind?"

She looked back, twisted her mouth into a teasing smile.

"Okay," he stalled for a second. Then: "Would you like to come in for coffee?"

She smiled, cheeks flushing. "Finally."

*

Alison thought of nothing but her misery as she tossed the last masked thug into the riot van. She heard him insult her under his breath, adding the c-word to 'slut' and 'whore' on the list of names she'd been called in the last three minutes, and it took all of her gargantuan strength not to squeeze his head until his skull creased. The cameras were watching, and it wouldn't look good. Not that it mattered to her anymore, but it would be selfish to give the new incumbent a hard time.

She turned to her audience. A rudimentary smile, the hands-on-hips stance they'd come to expect, and she threw an aching arm into the sky and glided towards the stars. Job done. The last memorable moment of her career had been for a foul-mouthed wideboy in a ski-mask to make her feel worthless. No statement, no voxpop, no fanfare, no farewell.

She soared higher. She thought about Clive, the prick the public knew as Manhammer, about how he'd thrown her out the night she'd told him she was done. The cape was everything to him, not because of any sense of duty or love for humanity, but because he loved the attention. Vanity was his weakness, narcissism his kryptonite. He adored the teenage girls fawning all over him as he flew overhead, and the middle aged women throwing their delicates, each pair an unsanitary declaration of lust he lapped up like a hungry dog, wrapped in corporate sponsorship and bullshit. She pictured him in his hideout with one of his conquests and hoped he caught something degenerative, something that ruined his healing factor, then cut himself shaving with the diamond razor she'd bought him for his birthday.

She was an idiot when she volunteered, young enough to think it was what she wanted. Why wouldn't it be? If life gives you lemons, you beat up the wretched for a living.

She hung in the lower veil of the clouds, gazing down at the lines of crawling dots of cars making their way home for the weekend. It was over. This was her last commute. Relief bathed her alongside the high-altitude breezes, cleansed her through the costume. So delightful was the feeling that she couldn't stop a tear falling, arcing down through the burgeoning rain shower where, unknown to her, it landed on an umbrella that didn't really belong to the one who carried it.

She fumbled in her utility belt for her phone, almost dropping her cigarettes a thousand feet into the traffic below. She had only started smoking since she put on the cape, hoping to get caught and released from duty, but scared of an entire world calling her trash or a bad role model, so she had never lit up publicly.

She scrolled the menu, found the initials 'MM' and dialled.

The Match Maker's voice always put her at ease. She had been the one Alison had gone to first, when she knew it was time to hang up the cape. Double-M took care of everything. She set up the replacement job, and Alison had been in for a few hours every day that week, getting to know the place, the responsibilities, finally putting into practice all the skills she had spent all her free time training for, in the brief moments when she was able to take off the mask. It wasn't all that different. Helping the afflicted and disenfranchised, occasionally being insulted and threatened, but generally making people better. To do that without every soul on earth staring right at you was more wonderful than she could describe. The nurse's uniform suited her much better anyway.

Alison thanked her for everything; the Match Maker had been the fourth Girlfight, back in the eighties, and had retired in much the same way. She understood everything, how the thrilling feeling of the super lifestyle could wane, and she took special care of every girl who took on the mantle, for however long they kept it, dozens of them now, each one eventually chasing the same dream. A life free of the limelight, away from the spandex and the spirit-gum. A normal, boring life, with husbands and children and mortgages and rent.

"One more thing," the Match Maker said as their conversation closed, and gave Alison some strange directions that would take her down the course of the river to a footbridge in the dark.

*

Monday rolled around in that inevitable way that Mondays tend to do, the memory of the weekend fast dwindling as the prospect of the next one crept inexorably closer. Trevor Trent found himself at work earlier than usual with an eagerness he thought forgotten. The reassuring boredom of routine was destined to continue.

Dexter and the Twins were bickering as ever; Ken and Dex were extolling the virtues of Journey's new singer as

Jimmy visibly became more worked up.

Pamela was on the phone. Trevor noticed that she had changed her desktop picture, to one of her and her family at a table in a colourful themed restaurant surrounded by servers in gaudy outfits, masks, capes and fake smiles. He nodded at the photo, his eyes asking the question of the day's success, hers answering with a withering roll.

Suzy made a quieter entrance and bade them sheepish good mornings. An awkward glance between her and Ken gave Trevor the answer he'd suspected. The details would come later; the silences would build to boiling point, the regret and the tears would burst out over drinks in the pub that coming Friday.

Trevor sat at his desk and opened his diary, pencilled something in: the reason he had marched to work a little happier than usual.

Pamela released the call, and logged the viewing appointment.

"Morning. Good weekend?"

Trevor shrugged. He had a story to tell, but was content for now to keep it his own.

"Not bad."

Pamela looked at the new booking she had just pencilled in to her diary. "Do you want to take that one? Twelve o'clock today."

"I can't, I'm already on a viewing."

"Whereabouts?"

"Handon Gardens."

"That's right by you, isn't it?" She crossed to him, peered at his diary. "Alison Jones. Bit of a dull name, isn't it?"

"She's a nurse," Trevor told her. "Meeting on her lunch hour."

Come noon, Pamela sat alone in the office, eating the sandwiches her daughter had helped her make before dashing off for school. She looked again at the photographs from their day out on Saturday, smiling as if she was looking at them for the first time.

She checked the news online, looking at the snaps of Captain Courage and Girlfight safely averting a train crash. Onlookers cheered, and nobody noticed that the heroine's hair was slightly different than it had been the week before, or that her bust was a little bigger.

Pamela recalled the first time she had put on that costume, already well-worn in by three others. It itched, and they had to take it in, just slightly, because her twenty-something puppy fat had yet to become muscle. She thought about the last time she took it off, the joy and the relief, the same way she later felt when she'd had the children. It was a strange and lonely life, all that flying around, constantly on camera. The only respite came from the secret identity, which always ended up being the thing you strived for. Saving a schoolbus of grateful children was no match for being able to talk to people about it, because you'd seen it on television like they had.

She kept her hand in, and they gave her a name; it was

easier to hide behind a name than a mask, and she was glad to help those girls once their time had passed, finding them homes if they needed, making the secret identity the one that mattered.

The Match Maker ate her sandwiches, looking at family photos with motherly contentment, as her lunch hour ticked away.

Down the block, Dexter, Kenny, Jimmy and Suzy visited the Dog & Parrot for a pub lunch peppered with innuendo and awkward silence.

Across town, a volunteer in a local charity shop unpacked two items from a plastic bag, a black skirt which was soon buried in a pile of other donated garments, and a well-worn umbrella.

Elsewhere, in a government funded penthouse, an eager young girl tentatively applied spirit-gum to her face and fixed a red mask in place, as a stylist cut her hair a few millimetres shorter to finally match an iconic, expected blond bob.

In Handon Gardens, Trevor Trent made tea in a flat that no longer smelled of old perfume, and handed a mug to a smiling brunette nurse who didn't like to smoke in front of her friends.

MY WRITER

My writer told me to come
　　so I did, to my core,
　　a gush of invisible ink.
Eyes, jade birds in flight;
　　hair, the shade of his favourite poem;
　　body, shaped like his memories of
　　a girl he knew next door;
　　heart, at his mercy.
He controls my every beat;
　　as good as good girls get,
　　and bad at his behest.
He gives me the feelings
　　he makes me want.
I pour onto his pages amongst
　　melded moments with men
　　that resemble the perfect he.
His pen drips, thrusts and dips
　　until I'm not a fiction, but infection,
　　the disease he gives to all
　　who think me.
I want to write my writer,
　　to give him the peace
　　he's given me.

ABOUT THE AUTHOR

Cameron Lincoln is a writer in a variety of genres and forms. He lives in England.

Find his official website at www.cameron-lincoln.com

Follow him on Twitter @Cameron_Lincoln and on Facebook at facebook.com/cameronlincolnwriter

Printed in Great Britain
by Amazon